Daniel O'Connor

Lough Derg

and its pilgrimages

Daniel O'Connor

Lough Derg
and its pilgrimages

ISBN/EAN: 9783337293642

Printed in Europe, USA, Canada, Australia, Japan

Cover: Foto ©Andreas Hilbeck / pixelio.de

More available books at **www.hansebooks.com**

LOUGH DERG

AND

ITS PILGRIMAGES.

WITH MAP AND ILLUSTRATIONS.

.

BY THE

REV. DANIEL O'CONNOR, C.C.,

PRIEST OF THE DIOCESE OF CLOGHER.

DUBLIN:

JOSEPH DOLLARD, PUBLISHER, 13 & 14 DAME-ST.

AND SOLD BY ALL BOOKSELLERS.

1879.

To the

MOST REV. JAMES DONNELLY, D.D.,

Bishop of Clogher

and

Guardian of the Sanctuary of Lough Derg,

This Little Volume

is

Most Respectfully Dedicated

by the

AUTHOR.

PREFACE.

IT has been long felt that a Handbook of the Pilgrimage of Lough Derg, giving an outline of its history, an accurate description of the place, as well as an account of the penitential exercises there practised, was a work, the want of which was admitted on all hands. To supply this want, however imperfectly, the present little volume has been written.

In its compilation I have received valuable aid and information from many kind friends, to whom I owe an acknowledgment of my most heartfelt gratitude. Foremost amongst these kind friends I must mention the Rev. John O'Hanlon, M.R.I.A., but for whose assistance and advice the present publication would very likely never have been prepared for the press. I have also to express my gratitude to the Right Rev. Dr. Graves, Protestant Bishop of Limerick, for a learned article on ancient inscriptions at Lough Derg, which his lordship, with the greatest kindness and condescension, permitted me to embody in this work. I am likewise

indebted to the Rev. John Francis Shearman,
M.R.I.A., for extracts from rare works, and also for
several learned and interesting notes from his own
pen. I have received valuable aid and information
from Mrs. Atkinson, of Fairview, Dublin ; from the
Rev. Peter M'Glone, President of St. M'Carten's
Seminary, Monaghan ; and from my obliging
friends, W. F. Wakeman, Esq., Enniskillen, and
the Rev. James M'Kenna, P.P., Brookeborough.

The illustrations were sketched on the spot, and
drawn on the wood by Mr. Wakeman, of Enniskillen, and engraved by that well-known lady-artist,
Mrs. Millard, of Dublin. The map of the lake,
annexed to this work, was prepared for the litho-
grapher by Mr. Wakeman.

Should this humble production receive from the
public that amount of favour and encouragement
which the subject itself deserves, it is my intention,
hereafter, to enlarge the work considerably by adding
additional matter, by inserting further engravings,
and by supplying a copious index.

Taking into account the difficulties and incon-
veniences under which I laboured in writing this

little work, the onerous and responsible duties of the sacred ministry, which occupied so much of my time and attention, the distance from public libraries, and the rather scanty materials for my subject within reach, the readers need not be surprised to find this work far from being as complete and exhaustive as we should wish. Whatever faults or inaccuracies may be pointed out to me, I shall most willingly correct them ; and should any additional information bearing on my subject be communicated to me, I shall thankfully acknowledge such information, and carefully preserve it for future publication.

And now, in bringing before the public, not without much anxiety and diffidence, this little production, I have only to add that if my humble efforts should contribute towards making more widely known the blessings and graces to be derived from a pilgrimage to Lough Derg, then the leisure moments, which I devoted to this subject, will not have been altogether spent in vain.

CORCAHAN, MONAGHAN,
December, 1878.

CONTENTS.

LIST OF ILLUSTRATIONS.

PILGRIMAGE OF LOUGH DERG.

CHAPTER I.

PRELIMINARY NOTICE.

IN this age of scepticism and unbelief, it is refreshing, indeed, to turn aside from the busy ways of the world, in order to contemplate the sanctuaries of religion—those bright green spots round which are encircled the sweetest associations and the most venerable traditions. To rescue them from the withering effects of neglect, or from the contemptuous scoff of the unbeliever, and to place before an admiring public their former glory, should be deemed a labour truly meritorious.

Every country in Europe can point out the mouldering ruins of church and cloister, overthrown and laid desolate by the destroying hand of war, or the no less relentless onslaught of heresy. But in no other country has so great destruction befallen the sacred edifices of religion as in Ireland—firstly, from the inroads of the Danish pirates;

and, lastly, from the law-established religion of England
in the sixteenth century, which visited the holy places of
religion with such fell destruction as neither Goth, Vandal,
nor Dane had ever paralleled.

Hence it comes that almost every parish in Ireland
presents ruins of either church or conventual establishment, which, in many instances, exhibit features of archi-
tectural design and grandeur in vain to be found in the
modern structures, which supply their places.

Nor did the ancient and extensive diocese of Clogher,
in point of ecclesiastical ruins, escape the general tide of
destruction which swept over the religious foundations of
Ireland. The ruins of the ecclesiastical city of Clogher,
of the foundations of St. Dagaeus MacCarroll at Inniskeen
(in the County Monaghan), of St. Fanchea at Rossory,
and of St. Molaisre at Devenish, are striking examples.
Of the Franciscan convents at Monaghan and Lisgoole,
not a stone remains upon a stone to mark their sites.
The ecclesiastical ruins at Clones even yet abundantly
attest the magnificence of its great abbey of SS. Peter
and Paul. Though these were the principal religious
houses within the diocese of Clogher (according to its
modern boundaries), yet there were others of less note,
not to speak of the parochial churches, most of which
shared the same sad fate at the hands of the Protestant
iconoclasts.

And how eloquently do not these desolate cloisters and
churches and places of pilgrimage and penance preach to
us, even in their ruins, of the prayer, piety and penance
of saint, monk and pilgrim ! The monumental ivy itself,

which is swathed round their walls, as if to preserve them
from the mouldering influence of time, waves mournfully
in the sobbing wind over their ruins, seeming still to re-
echo the solemn strains of the pious inmates who used to
chaunt within those hallowed precincts the never-ending
hymn of praise and thanksgiving. Cold, indeed, must
the spectator be whose heart is not moved at beholding
those sanctuaries of religion, on which time has left the
deep traces of its action—whose heart is not carried back
by the spirit that breathes of these holy places to the
time when prayer and sacrifice were being offered up to
heaven from within those walls !

And, as there is nothing so consoling to the human
heart as the sweetening influences of religion—those
purifying delights of the senses and of the soul—so there
is no other reflection or study more refreshing to the
mind than the consideration of the holy places of religion,
with the records of the virtue and piety of their saintly
inmates.

Of all the ecclesiastical institutions of our country, none
can lay such claim to the homage of our veneration as
the holy places of pilgrimage—those places purified by
the prayer and penances of saints, blessed by their labours,
sanctified by the sweet odour of their virtues, and consecrated anew to that original purity which the world
enjoyed before the Fall. But of the many places of
pilgrimage which have flourished throughout Ireland
since the introduction of Christianity, the sanctuary of
Lough Derg, in Donegal, generally entitled " St. Patrick's
Purgatory," has always occupied the most prominent place,

and alone merited the proud distinction of being regarded
as the national pilgrimage of Ireland.   And so celebrated
was it, that during the Middle Ages it enjoyed a Continental fame.   Justly, therefore, writes the Rev. Sylvester
Malone, in his *Church History of Ireland*, "There was a
time, and pilgrimage to Lough Derg was scarcely less
famous than that to the shrine of the Apostle St. James
at Compostella, in Spain."

The precise date and origin of this pilgrimage, its
founder, the *locale* of its purgatorial cave or cell—these
and many other points in connection with the history of
Lough Derg remain involved in considerable obscurity,
affording to the future historian of the place ample grounds
for labour and research.   The destruction of this religious
establishment by the so-called Reformation, and the
"Dark Ages" of Irish history consequent thereon, have
rendered it extremely difficult to make out anything like
a clear, connected and reliable outline regarding the
history of—

> "That dim lake,
> Where sinful souls their farewell take
> Of this vain world, and half-way lie
> In death's cold shadow ere they die."

To do adequate justice to this subject, more abundant
materials and more patient investigation than the writer
of these pages can hope to command, would be necessarily
required.   But, since the subject of pilgrimages has of
late awakened a spirit of religious fervour in many lands,
and since the shrines of religion in Continental countries
are described in countless works, while "the cold chain

of silence" still hangs round the sanctuaries of holy
Ireland, I hope I may claim indulgence in laying before
the public my limited store of information regarding
Ireland's greatest pilgrimage—the sanctuary of Lough
Derg. And should my observations tend towards popu-
larizing and extending the knowledge of this pilgrimage,
which dates back through the mists of centuries—even
to the very infancy of the faith in Ireland—the labour
entailed shall be truly a labour of love to me.

Before entering on the immediate subject of this work,
namely, an historical and descriptive outline of the pilgrimage and its penitential exercises, I think it right
briefly to explain the nature and origin, or the philosophy,
so to call it, of pilgrimages.

----◆----

CHAPTER II.

ON THE NATURE AND ORIGIN OF PILGRIMAGES—THEIR GROWTH—SUPPRESSION AND REVIVAL.

HERE is a feeling—a natural conviction—
deeply implanted in the heart of man that
all places are not equally adapted for the
service of God ; that certain places, owing
to their position and other circumstances,
possess a special natural fitness for rendering
homage and adoration to the God of Nature.
For this reason mountains have been usually
selected by the servants of God, on account of their being
so adapted for the communings of the soul with the

Creator, for their being more free from the iniquities of man, nearer heaven, and conveying a more sublime idea of the Divine power and majesty.   And thus, the mountain region of Lough Derg, in Donegal, of Croagh-Patrick, in Western Connaught, of St. Brendan's mountain, in Kerry, not to adduce many other similar instances, were peculiarly and naturally adapted for the performance of holy exercises.

In a work by one of the Oratorian Fathers, which is entitled *Holy Places; their Sanctity and Authenticity*, this idea is thus vividly expressed—"In such places" (which have this natural selection of place) "Nature discloses her mysteries, echoes of contemplation arise to the Author of Nature, and there the noblest faculties of the soul become, so to say, spiritualized.   We know that the gloom of forests, the solemnity of night, the weird-like mystery of caverns, the awfulness of storms, the majesty of mountains—all have their place with the devout servant of God in lifting his soul beyond this passing world to his home beyond the stars."

In the wonderful harmony and order which pervade the universe we find everything possessing its own order, place and fitness.   Even the religious orders themselves, which are the most lively reflection, as they are the most active exponents, of the Divine lessons of our Blessed Lord and of His counsels of perfection—each possesses, in its own sphere of life and action, a certain local fitness, as it is expressed in the following distich—

> "*Bernardus valles, montes Benedictus amabat*
> *Oppida Franciscus, magnas Ignatius urbes.*"

This fitness of place for God's service is manifested in different ways. "At sundry times and in divers manners God spoke to our fathers."—Heb., i. 1. It is manifested by visions, such as that of Jacob; by the visits of angels—and thus the place where the angels conversed familiarly with Abraham was holy; by apparitions, such as that of the burning bush; by miracles, &c.

Now, it is but natural to expect that men should have set apart places thus favoured for the purpose of prayer and sacrifice; and that in the lapse of time a network of traditions and pious associations and sacred ceremonies having continued in such places, should have rendered them truly holy. Natural fitness, or, as St. Ignatius designates it, "composition of place," is not enough that a place should be esteemed holy. It must also receive some designation of sanctity or consecration from God or His chosen servants.

Though God is the author and source of consecration, yet He has frequently deputed angels and men as the instruments of consecration; and though we highly revere places blessed by angels and men, yet we retain the highest veneration for such places as receive their consecration immediately from God, and bear, as it were, the impress and sign-manual of God Himself. God frequently makes use of the saints, His servants, to consecrate places to His special service. For the saint is the living tabernacle of the Holy Ghost; he everywhere carries about with him the sweet odour of his virtues; his friends love and cherish his memory, and revere, for his sake, the holy places with which are associated his pious actions, his charity, his prayer and penance. And, even after he quits the scene of this life, the memory and sweet attractions of his virtue draws them around his grave, so that his grave comes to be regarded as possessed of a special character of holiness.

And thus not only the natural fitness of the place itself, but also prayer, penance, pious custom, sacred ceremonies, some selection of place by God or His chosen servants, or some other special manifestation of consecration, go to give a place a distinctive character of sanctity, and render it a fit resort for pilgrimage.

Such holy places there have been from the beginning, in which men were wont familiarly to converse with God, as did Moses on Mount Sinai. And of these sacred places very many have become lost to memory, such as the places esteemed sacred by the nomadic tribes in the desert; such as the places dignified by the visions of Job and the Prophets—nay, even many of the places rendered notable by the miracles of our Lord and of His Apostles. And thus, since man's life on earth is itself a pilgrimage, there have always been places set apart in a special manner for the service of God, in which all that is heavenly in man could find a sanctuary wherein to commune with and draw nearer to God.

At all times there have been pilgrimages, and amongst all nations. Even the Pagans had their temples, where they came to adore their false gods. The Druids also had their sacred groves. The Mahometans make pilgrimage to the tomb of the arch-impostor, Mahomet. In the Old Law there were Levitical cities and cities of

refuge, which God set apart for Himself in Israel. The
Jewish people, also, journeyed at fixed periods to their
temple at Jerusalem. But it was in the New Law, when
religion received its full perfection and development, that
the practice of pilgrimage became an established exercise
of religion. The holy places at Jerusalem, and the other
places made sacred in connection with the life and passion
of our Blessed Lord, occupied the foremost place in these
pious journeys. Next in order rank the shrines of the
Madonna. After these comes the tomb of the Apostles
in Rome ; while next in importance follow the chief
places of pilgrimage in every country—in Ireland, St.
Patrick's Purgatory holding the most prominent place.

The Abbé Receveur, in his *Discours sur l'Histoire
Ecclesiastique,* writes thus regarding the development of
pilgrimages :—" One can readily perceive how the spirit
of devotion came to attract people to the places sanctified
by the presence and death of the Saviour. This respect
for the holy places and for the tombs of the Apostles gave
birth to pilgrimages. They had commenced in the first
ages ; and we know that St. Alexander, who became
Bishop of Jerusalem, had come from Cappadocia to visit
the holy places. But the liberty of the Church and the
discovery of the true Cross rendered pilgrimages more easy
and more frequent. St. Cyril of Jerusalem, St. Jerome,
and the historian, Sozomene, testify that, during the fourth
century, the holy places were visited by multitudes of
pilgrims, who had recourse to them from all the nations
of the world. This devotion continued even after Pales-
tine had fallen into the hands of the Mussulmans. As to

the tombs of saints and martyrs, people came to them
even from a great distance, not only on the day of their
festival, but also at other times. Everyone knows how
celebrated had come to be pilgrimage to Rome, to the
tombs of the holy Apostles ; to Tours, to the tomb of
St. Martin ; of St. James at Compostella, &c. Princes,
bishops, monks and religious of every order, showed
great zeal for this practice of devotion. The usage also
introduced itself, little by little, in the eighth century, of
imposing pilgrimage by way of penance. The Council
of Chalons, held in 813, under Charlemagne, approved
of this practice ; but, at the same time, warned against
the abuses of it."

The Ages of Faith were the "golden age" of pilgrimages. And we are told by Hallam, a very prejudiced
writer, that, during the eleventh century, more pilgrims
went to Jerusalem than at any previous time. And the
same writer, speaking of the Crusades, says, "They were
martial pilgrimages on an enormous scale."

The Church has always guarded her places of pilgrimage with the most jealous care. Next to ecclesiastical
doctrines and persons, there is nothing that she defends
with severer penalties than these sanctuaries. In this
cause she has enacted laws and rules, and issued her
censures against their transgressors. In this cause she
spares not the life, the labour and the treasures of her
children. With this object has she founded religious
orders, orders of knighthood, and preached the Crusades.

The interest created by the various philosophic and
scholastic systems, by the invention of arts and sciences,

by the discovery of new lands and new peoples, had, greatly to the disadvantage of the holy places of religion, for a long period engaged the attention of men. Above all, the religious disruption of the sixteenth century, the upheaval of society, the wars and countless calamities consequent thereon, rendered it extremely difficult, if not in some places impossible, for organized pilgrimages to take place as of old. But as the passion inspired by these inventions and discoveries has begun to subside, and as the religious animosities, which have been un-happily so long-lived, are at length disappearing before the mellowing influence of time and enlightenment, the world, always athirst for novelty, is again fast turning its attention to the study of the early Christian ages, of the early Christian practices, and of the sacred places of religion. And thus the early pilgrimages, which were suppressed by the Reformation, are at length springing, phœnix-like, from their ashes, and bursting forth with renewed life into the light of day, as the seed, buried deep in the earth during the winter, will spring into light and robe itself in verdure when the storms shall have passed away.

CHAPTER III.

LOVE OF THE IRISH FOR THE HOLY PLACES OF PILGRIMAGE
—THEIR MULTIPLICATION — STONE CROSSES — HOLY
WELLS—ST. PATRICK'S PURGATORY.

F Ireland we must say that her children were always remarkable for the pilgrim-spirit, the great number of places of pilgrimage throughout the country being the best proof of this. In its zeal for the holy places, the early Irish Church had spread the network of sanctity over the whole extent of the land—Lough Derg, Clonmacnoise, Arran of the Saints, Croagh-Patrick, Glendalough, and a number of other sanctuaries, were frequented by crowds of pilgrims.

And not only were the temples of religion the scene of these pious journeys, but also the saint's cell and place of penance, his grave, the different objects blessed by him, such as crosses and holy wells, became special centres of attraction in the eyes of a devout and affectionate people.

Pilgrimage to crosses and holy wells was once, and in some degree still continues to be, a very popular and cherished devotion amongst the Catholics of Ireland. These crosses and holy wells were, in many cases, blessed by the saints whose names they bear; in others, dedicated to them and placed under their invocation. On the vigil or festival of the saint, whose name they bore, the faithful made pilgrimage to them, and went through a certain course of devotional exercises.

In an ancient Life of St. Columbkille, preserved in the leabhan bpeac, it is said of him, "He blessed three hundred miraculous crosses; he blessed three hundred wells, which were constant."

The fact of the multiplication of these holy places in Ireland, as well as the hostility shown towards them by the reformed creed, made it difficult to frequent them; and thus many of these cherished places have come to be forgotten, together with many interesting circumstances and traditions connected with them. The extermination of the old race, and the introduction of new settlers, with new habits and ideas, had also contributed to hasten the decline of this time-honoured practice. Abuses also crept in, having their origin in the penal times, which rendered these gatherings objectionable to the ecclesiastical authorities; and, in consequence, many of these pilgrimages were discontinued. "Much, however," writes the Rev. Dean Cogan, in his *History of the Diocese of Meath*, " of the poetry of religion, of the chivalry of lively faith—much that was grand and romantic in the heartfelt devotion of a truly Catholic people—is intertwined with the history of the Holy Wells of Ireland."

The oldest existing institution of the Irish Church is the pilgrimage of St. Patrick's Purgatory. It forms a connecting link between the days of St. Patrick and the present day. The penitential exercises of this pilgrimage constitute the most venerable, and, perhaps, the only authorized surviving instance of the early Irish religious exercises and penitential discipline—a discipline under which had flourished so many saints and scholars. This

pilgrimage has been always regulated and conducted by
the ecclesiastical authorities. It has never been interrupted, at least for any notable time. And even " whilst
everywhere else throughout the kingdom," writes Bishop
Hugh MacMahon, in 1714, " the ecclesiastical functions
have ceased, on account of the prevailing persecution, in
this island, as if it were placed in another orb, the exercise
of religion is free and public, which is ascribed to a
special favour of Divine Providence and to the merits of
St. Patrick."

During the middle ages poetic imagination and romance
had invented a very exaggerated and misleading picture
of St. Patrick's Purgatory. That it was so called because
of any similarity between its exercises and the sufferings
of the purgatorial state hereafter, or because of its local
proximity to it, no one will for a moment admit.

A plausible reason for its being called St. Patrick's
Purgatory, is given in a Louvain treatise of the seventeenth
century, called the *Mirror of Penance*. It is there said
how St. Patrick removed from the abstractions of the
world into that gloomy ᴅᴇᴘᴄ, or cave ; and that he there
prayed that the pains of purgatory might be revealed to
him. His request was granted. Patrick was so much
awed by this vision, that he departed from the cave, and
ordered that henceforward the island should be made a
terrestrial purgatory, where sinners could atone for their
sins by prayer and fasting.

The origin of the name, however, is sufficiently accounted
for from the fact that St. Patrick selected this island for
the performance of those deeds of penance for which he

was so remarkable, and that so many saints and pious pilgrims imitated his example; the island in consequence being called St. Patrick's Purgatory, or place of penance. This meaning is thus conveyed in the following sweet lines, taken from Denis Florence M'Carthy's translation of Calderon's *Purgatory of St. Patrick :—*

" Where although 'twas plain they suffered,
  Still they looked with joyous faces,
  Wore a peaceable appearance,
  Uttered no impatient accents ;
  But with moistened eyes uplifted
  Towards the heavens, appeared imploring
  Pity, and their sins lamenting—
  This in truth was purgatory."

It is even stated, but so far as I know gratuitously, that the original St. Patrick's Purgatory was on Croagh-Patrick ; and that the Augustinian Canons had dignified with that imposing title their own retreat at Lough Derg, somewhere during the middle ages.

Though the name itself is but a matter of secondary importance, yet in proving, as we shall endeavour to do, in the course of this work, that the institution at Lough Derg was founded by our Apostle, St. Patrick, and that it has continued as a place of retirement and penance since his day ; then it will be abundantly clear how reasonable is the designation it has received, and how unfounded is the assertion made by Dr. Lanigan and others, for the purpose, no doubt, of lessening the character and antiquity of this penitential retreat.

CHAPTER IV.

TEMPLECARN—LOUGH DERG—ORIGIN OF THE NAME—
THE LAKE—ITS SCENERY AND SURROUNDINGS.

OUGH DERG, the scene of the time-honoured pilgrimage of St. Patrick's Purgatory, is situated in the parish of Templecarn, barony of Tyrhugh, county of Donegal, and diocese of Clogher. It is distant between three and four miles from the neat little town of Pettigoe, which is a station on the Bundoran branch of the Enniskillen and Londonderry railway.

In the hypothesis that the pilgrim will proceed to Lough Derg by way of Pettigoe (which appears to derive its name from a clan, called ᵮᵿⁿⁿ˔ⁱᵽ ᵽᵉᴀᴅᴀᴄʰᴀⁿ, that whilom held sway in this locality), he will pass convenient to the old churchyard of Templecarn, which gives name to the parish, within which lies Lough Derg. This churchyard stands on the brow of a hill in the townland of Carn, nearly midway between Pettigoe and Lough Derg, and some distance to the left of the modern road leading towards the lake.

Of Templecarn there is found but the following notice in the Annals of the Four Masters:—" 1497. O'Donnell, *i.e.*, Hugh Roe, resigned his lordship on the calends of June, being Friday, at Templecarn, in the Termon, in consequence of the dissensions of his sons." Down to this period the church of the Termon was on Saints'

Island; but, whether in consequence of the edict of
Pope Alexander VI., which was issued in the early part of
the same year 1497, or for the greater convenience of
those who resided on these termon-lands, Templecarn was
erected towards the latter part of the fifteenth century,
and afterwards became a parish church. When the
surrounding district came to be "planted" with Protestant settlers, they appropriated this church to their own
use, after the fashion so generally followed at the time.
Of this old church there are hardly any traces left. The
walls have completely disappeared, and we can with
difficulty trace its outline and dimensions by means of
the hollow space which marks the interior of the church,
and the raised surface, where stood its walls. The site
of the old church is still discernible in the centre of the
graveyard. It measured 66 feet in length by about 22 in
width.

The churchyard of Templecarn has been used for very
many years as a burial-place by Protestants and Catholics
alike. It is enclosed by a substantial wall, and
approached by a convenient entrance and gateway. It
is completely studded with tombstones of every variety,
many of them as old as the sixteenth century, with raised
characters, or in *alto-relievo*, as was the custom during the
sixteenth and seventeenth centuries. The arms and
mottoes of the Johnstons and other local families are
inscribed on several of these tombstones. Some of the
monuments are certainly very elegant, and bespeak a
considerable amount of native art in the locality. In
the body of the old church some of the tombstones are

c

almost buried in the earth; and I have no doubt but
that others more ancient are completely hidden from
view by the accumulation of earth, owing to the great
number of interments.

Templecarn Churchyard.

In Templecarn churchyard may be seen a very ancient
Celtic cross. The tradition is that it was transferred from
Saints' Island, and erected in the midst of the graves of
those who were drowned by the boat accident on Lough
Derg in 1795. That distinguished antiquarian, W. F.
Wakeman, Esq., of Enniskillen, says it must be as old as
the ninth century at least. It is supposed that this was
one of the termon crosses which marked the limits of

Termon-Dabheoc. But that it is much smaller, it exactly resembles in form the termon crosses of Tullagh, near Loughlinstown, Co. Dublin. This cross measures in shaft 1 foot 4 inches in length of pedestal sunk in the ground ; from pedestal to top of shaft, 2 feet ; width of the arms, 11 inches. A portion of the circlet has been broken off the left side; and the head of the cross itself, including the arms, has been also broken, but remains in its place so so long as the cross is kept in an upright stationary position.

At the western corner of this churchyard may be seen (as shown on the illustration of Templecarn already inserted) the finest specimen I have witnessed of a *bohogue*, in a good state of preservation, and having an altar-table of stone. These *bohogues*, or huts, which afforded shelter and accommodation merely for the altar and the priest, were commonly availed of throughout the north of Ireland, even within the memory of those living, for the celebration of the Sacred Mysteries. This *bohogue* is sheltered by an arched or hood-like covering of stone. Its measurements are :—Height from ground to centre of arch, 7½ feet; width at entrance, about 6 feet ; depth, 7½ feet ; depth of altar-table, 2½ feet.

On some of the monuments within this graveyard may be seen a remnant, or imitation, of that curious interlacing, known as *opus Hibernicum*, for which the ancient Irish monuments are so remarkable.

From Templecarn may be had an extensive view of Lough Erne and its islands, with the Fermanagh and Leitrim mountains in the background. There is neither tree nor shrub within or around this churchyard. Past

this churchyard led the ancient roadway to Saints'
Island; so that we may safely conjecture that before the
altar of Templecarn many a weary and footsore pilgrim
to Lough Derg had offered a prayer in passing. In the
neighbourhood of Templecarn the only objects of antiquarian interest I know of are strange megalithic remains
in the townland of Tamlaght; also a holy well at a place
named Cullion.

It is generally supposed that Lough Derg was known
in ancient Erin under the name of Fionloch, or the fair
lake. That there was another lake of the same name,
where lower Lough Erne unfolds its spreading waters,
would appear from the following extract taken from
O'Flaherty.

"*Fordremanus, Finloch, Lochlorgan, Stagna vetusta,
Quos, quam culta prius, fudit Ierna lacus.*"

The supposition that Lough Derg was anciently called
Fionloch appears to rest on the authority of the legend
regarding St. Patrick and the serpent; setting that legend
aside, I see no reason for denying that it was always called
Lough Derg.

There are two different opinions to account for the
meaning of the denomination, Lough Derg. The first is
founded on a legend, which goes on to say that a frightful
serpent inhabited this locality, and spread terror and
destruction far and wide; that St. Patrick, being come into
the district, put the serpent to death; that the waters of
the lake were dyed of a reddish colour by its blood; and
thus the name of the lake, which was hitherto called
ꝼﻪoɲn, fair or clear, came to be called ᴅeﻪᵹs, which

signifies red. This legend, though in substance the same,
is differently told by O'Donnellan, in the notes to his
edition of the *Four Masters;* by Dr. O'Donovan, in his
Donegal Letters, preserved in the Royal Irish Academy ;
and by Mr. Wakeman, in a short notice and sketch of
Lough Derg, published in the *Pictorial World*, August
28th, 1875.

This derivation of the name is not admitted by
O'Donovan, who pronounces himself quite incredulous as
to these legends and local traditions. He says : " I am
quite satisfied the name of the lake is not *Loch-Dearg*,
i.e. Red Lough, but *Loch-Deirc*, which means the Lough
of the Cave." This opinion is greatly sustained from the
way in which it is found written in early notices of it. It
is called Loch Gerc and Logh Gerg, and the district in
which it lay was called *Glinn Deirg*. This construction,
also, is that adopted by the Rev. John Francis Shearman
of Howth, in his *Loca Patriciana*.

That the waters of Lough Derg bear a reddish tinge to
this very day is beyond all doubt, which, if it be not
attributable to the legend aforesaid, is easily accounted
for by reason of its waters flowing over a boggy or
heathy surface. When agitated by a storm the water
of the lake becomes very muddy ; but when the lake
becomes calm again, the water is clear, and very pa-
latable. The colour of the water, as also its agreeable
taste when taken in a warm state, gave rise to its receiving, by a very appropriate fiction, the name of "wine.'
Formerly this "wine" was the only beverage taken by
the pilgrims while they remained "on station." Till

recently the large copper, in which this "wine" was boiled, lay rusting in a corner of the island, the modern innovation of boarding-houses and tea-kettles having discarded its occupation. Being such a useful relic of the past, it has been dignified with being marked on the Ordnance Survey Map of the place; and hence, though there is now no trace of it to be seen, its memory is not destined soon to perish.

Reserving for another place a description of the road leading from Pettigoe to Lough Derg, as well as of the other routes from Castlederg and Donegal, I shall now briefly describe the lake, its islands, its situation and surroundings.

Lough Derg is a lonely sheet of water, extending from north to south, about six miles in length. Its greatest width from Pŏrtcreevy to the River Derg is fully four miles. It is thirteen miles in circuit, and covers an area of 2,140 statute acres. It is surrounded by a chain of mountains, some of which rise to a considerable elevation above the level of the lake. The Rev. Caèsar Otway, in his *Sketches in Donegal,* and other writers after him, from whom we should expect a more impartial description, if not so graphic, say that there is no grandeur in the scenery of Lough Derg, no variety in the outline, the mountains without elevation, neither tree nor green spot to relieve this sombre scenery. A more unfair or distorted picture the greatest enemy of the place could hardly give. Here, indeed, you have all the charms of Highland scenery, and much in addition. The extensive sheet of water, with rocky shores and numerous islands, is all that can be admired. In the background the mountains are of considerable and varying elevation. And though heath is here the prevailing robe of nature, yet occasional patches of trees and bushes, with many a sunny slope and green sward and wooded island, relieve the scenery of its stern and wild aspect. But above and beyond all, the traditions and associations of the place impart to it an attraction and charm which no beauty of scenery could supply.

The lake is about 450 feet above the level of the sea ; while the highest surrounding mountains are Crockinnagoe, to the south-east of the lake, 1,194 feet ; Ardmore and Ougtadreen towards the north, 1,086 and 1,071 feet high respectively ; the mountains to the south and west not reaching an elevation of 1,000 feet.

The chain of hills towards the south of the lake forms the watershed between northern and southern Ulster. The streams flowing south of this chain of hills meet the Termon river at Pettigoe, thence flowing into Lough Erne ; while the streams flowing northward empty into Lough Derg, and thence into the sea at Lough Foyle.

"The basin of the lake is a huge quarry of the metamorphic rock, known as mike slate, or schist, upheaved in ages azoic by some fiery agent, so that the stratifaction is now almost perpendicular to the surface. It crops up all round the shore, and through the lake into numerous rocky islets and hidden reefs, whose projecting points are sharp as iron spikes, and render the navigation of the lake a matter of great caution."*

* From an article in the *Irish Monthly*, January Number, 1878.

Lough Derg consists of two large sheets of water, which may be designated the upper and lower lakes. The upper lake is connected with the lower by means of three channels formed by Saints' Island and an islet lying north-east of it, called by that name of bad omen, "The Wildgoose Lodge." The principal streams flowing into the lake are called the rivers Fluchlynn and Barderg, which fall into Lough Derg at its north-western extremity. The outlet is called the River Derg, which issues from the lake at the north-eastern shore, and pursues its winding way till it mingles with the ocean at Lough Foyle.

Lough Derg is bespangled with numerous and pretty islands, some crowned with stunted trees, some bared to the mountain breezes. The principal of these islands are Inishgoosk, *alias* Bilberry Island; Saints' Island, Station Island, Prior's Island, Allingham's Island, Ash Islands, Boat Islands, near the quay; Stormy Islands, Kelly's Isles, Goat Islands, near the River Fluchlynn; Derg More Island. Derg Beg Island, Trough Island and Bull's Island. Besides these, there are a good many other islets with no particular designation ; and which, with few exceptions, are mere groups of barren rocks, where cranes, cormorants and sea-gulls nestle, imparting by their wild and plaintive screams a lonely and romantic charm to this island hermitage. In the above enumeration Saints' Island seems to have been sometimes called St Fintan's Island, and very often St. Dabheoc's Island. Inishgoosk would appear to be the most ancient name at present attached to any of these islands ; and it may be taken to mean the

island of the cove, or creek, on account of its formation
at its western extremity.

In point of extent of area, Inishgoosk is the largest of
the islands of Lough Derg, containing 13 acres 2 roods
24 perches ; Saints' Island ranks next, containing 10 acres
1 rood 16 perches; while Station Island only ranks
eleventh, as it contains only 3 roods and 26 perches, statute
measure. In point of history, however, and celebrity,
Saints' Island occupies the first place, Station Island
second ; while the other islands of Lough Derg present
no particular interest, or attraction to the historian or
pilgrim.

During the station season Lough Derg presents from
all points of view, 'mid its dreary solitude of mountain
and moorland, a singularly charming and picturesque
prospect, with the neat churches and presbytery and inns
on Station Island—

" White as a swan on the breast of its waters."

And of this scenery memory will treasure up a picture,
upon which to look back during the cold and wintry days
of life. Here the eye is filled with the charms of
mountain, lake and island. The step of the pilgrim
becomes, as it were, spellbound ; for, the island, towards
which he journeys, is, as he must instinctively feel, sacred
ground—

" So like a temple doth it stand, that there
The heart's first impulse is to prayer."

The mind conjures up from the distant past many
conjectures regarding this island penitentiary. The finger

of God is truly visible in its destination and natural apti-
tude. The surrounding mountains stand like huge
sentinels round this island sanctuary, forming, as it were,
a barrier against the contaminating influences of the outer
world.

Round this island pilgrimage the waves dash and roar—
meet emblem of the troublous billows of the world, and
of the storms which beset the soul ; while the heart of the
pilgrim is lured from the wild and desolate prospect on
every side to the star-set firmament, which beckons
upwards to the eternal hills—the true home of the
pilgrim.

CHAPTER V.

SAINTS' ISLAND—ITS OUTLINE AND APPEARANCE—SITE OF ST. DABHEOC'S MONASTERY.

ABOUT two miles north of Station Island
lies Saints' Island, anciently called
Oileán-na-naoṁ, and more anciently still,
St. Dabheoc's* Island. In pre-Reforma-
tion times there stood on Saints' Island a
venerable convent of Augustinians; and, at
least down to the year 1497, this island would
appear to have been the place of pilgrimage.
The island is like a ring in form, and rises on all sides
in gentle acclivity from the lake, its highest elevation
being about forty feet above the level of the lake.

---

*This name, " Dabheoc," is usually pronounced as if written *Davoc.*

Saints' Island bears evident traces of agriculture, and
of having been turned to profitable account in the days
when the Canons Regular of St. Augustine were denizens
of the place. The soil of the island is rank and loamy,
and seems to have partaken of the ruin which has visited
with such destruction its holy cloisters and churches. It
is quite overgrown with coarse grass, with ferns and
rushes; and in some parts of it a stunted covering of
heather indicates that it has, to some extent, returned to
its original state of wildness. The ruins of the sacred
enclosures, monastery, churches and cemetery, are overgrown with luxuriant weeds. The island has very few
trees or shrubs, if we except some slender trees of mountain ash, and some whitethorn bushes, which are really
worth observing, as they are hoar with antiquity. These
bushes are sparsely scattered over the island, but at its
eastern extremity a dense cluster of them overshadows the
debris of the buildings; and, judging from the gray, dank
moss adhering to their branches, they appear to date from
the time these buildings were demolished.

On the southern slope of the island were situated the
convent gardens, as we may plainly infer from the
enclosures, as well as from the superior fertility of the soil.
During the winter season these gardens present a more
marked contrast for their verdure; and herbs and flowers
are known to grow here, which are not found elsewhere through these islands and mountains.

The eastern half of the island was laid out in fields,
as the remains of the earthen fences or enclosures denote.
These fences are inhabited by a numerous colony of

rabbits, of different colours, brown, white and black, that skip about in every direction, and in a variety of ways contribute their own little best " to lend enchantment to the scene."

The western half of the island appears to have been used as a " common " for pasture, as it is not intersected by fences, though here also the furrowed surface presents indications of its having yielded to the beneficent sway of the spade and ploughshare.

The grass and hay grown on Saints' Island are said to be so rank and unsavoury as to be very noxious to cattle. Formerly, I have been informed, cattle and sheep were put to pasture on it, till the mortality which set in amongst them awakened their owners to the dangers of the situation. And thus, fortunately, the sacred precincts and ruins on the island are no longer trampled upon, dishonoured and profaned by the beasts of the field, which in other places have occasioned such injury to the ancient monuments of our country.

In the early ages of the faith in Ireland there appears to have prevailed a custom, borrowed from the pagan period, of erecting a circular earthen fort or enclosure convenient to, or around the religious houses. Thus, in Father O'Hanlon's *Life of St. Fanchea*, we read of her brother, St. Endeus, having with his own hands raised round his sister's nunnery, at Rossory, a large muᵽ, or earthwork, strengthened by deep circular fosses, the remains of which are still to be seen. And Mr. Wakeman, in his *Antiquities of Devenish*, says that nearly all the primitive church sites in Fermanagh bear traces

of such circumvallations. The writer of the present
subject, from his own personal observation of some of
these sites, can fully endorse Mr. Wakeman's statement.
Near the Abbey of Devenish stood a strongly-fortified
ράth, remains of which are still evident. The same may
be said of Rossory, Inniskeen, &c. Outside Fermanagh
the same custom also prevailed. At Clogher and Clones
religious houses were founded, for economy sake, near forts,
of which we have sufficient evidence for saying that they
were erected during the pre-Christian period of our country.

On Saints' Island, also, the visitor will perceive a
circular earthwork of this class, on the very summit of the
island, and to the west of the monastery and cemetery.
The diameter of this enclosure measures about twenty yards.
A part of this circular earthwork has been intersected by
the cemetery, which lies to the east of it; but as much of
it, fortunately, still remains as to leave no doubt whatever
as to the character and object of this primitive work. It
seems strange, indeed, that this interesting object escaped
the notice of the Ordnance Survey party, and even of
O'Donovan himself, who visited the island on the 28th
of October, 1835. It is much to be regretted that
O'Donovan did not devote more of his time and attention
to this locality ; as, with his rare knowledge, much that
is now hopelessly lost might have been brought to light.
He came, as we said, on the 28th of October, and on
Hallow-Eve following he wrote, from Ballyshannon, an account of his visit to the lake, having derived, as he jocosely
states, no benefit from his ευραγ save a severe cold.

Within this fort on Saints' Island, or, at any rate, in the

cemetery adjoining, it is not too much of conjecture to say that the monastery founded here by St. Dabheoc, in the days of St. Patrick, stood ; and that here his order flourished till the time of the Danish invasion.

The object of these forts seems to have been to shelter and protect the religious houses against the storm, to serve as places of observation wherein watch and vigil might be kept, and as keeps, or fortifications against marauding parties. That no remains of the original monastery are extant is not to be wondered at, seeing that most of the edifices belonging to this period were built of wood. On this subject Dr. Lanigan, in his *Ecclesiastical History of Ireland* (vol. iv., p. 391), writes :—

"Prior to the twelfth century the general fashion was to erect their buildings of wood, a fashion which in great part continues to this day in several parts of Europe. As, consequently, their churches also were usually built of wood, it cannot be expected that there should be any remains of such churches at present."

With regard to the plan and arrangement of the ancient Irish Monasteries, Dr. Petrie (*Round Towers*, p. 416) remarks :—"It is clear that in the earliest monastic establishments in Ireland, the abbot, clergy and monks, had each their separate cells, which served as habitations; and that such other houses as the house for the accommodation of strangers, the kitchen, &c., were all separate edifices, surrounded by a *cashel*, or circular wall, and forming a kind of monastery, or ecclesiastical town, like those of the Christians in the East, and known among the Egyptians by the name of *Laura*."

There is an air of loneliness and desolation about Saints' Island, which is truly affecting. Silence, still as death, reigns round these holy precincts, where once the prayer of the pilgrim, the pious chant of the monks, 'mid ceremony and sacrifice, resounded. Of this island we may repeat with truth what was said of " Arran of the Saints," that the living God alone knows the number of holy persons who here await their final resurrection.

Standing on this holy island, where stood the monastery of St. Dabheoc, where stood the sanctuary of Saint Patrick's Purgatory, which during the middle ages became " the most famous shrine of penance and purification in Western Europe," the following sweet lines recur to memory :—

> " God of this Irish isle,
>   Sacred and old,
>   Bright in the morning smile
>   Is the lake's fold ;
>   Here where thy saints have trod,
>   Here where they prayed,
>   Hear me, O saving God !
>   May I be saved !"

CHAPTER VI.

ST. PATRICK AT LOUGH DERG—MEMORIALS OF HIM PRE-
SERVED THERE—ST. DABHEOC—HIS GENEALOGY—HIS
AUSTERITIES—HIS PROPHECY REGARDING ST. COLUMBA
—RECORDS OF HIM AT LOUGH DERG.

IT is a subject much controverted among Irish hagiologists whether St. Patrick, our national Apostle, had ever visited Lough Derg; and if so, whether the pilgrimage takes its origin from him, or from another saint of the same name, called Patrick Junior, or the Abbot Patrick, who flourished, according to the authority of Sir James Ware, about the year 850.

And though we may admit with O'Donovan, that we do not possess "any respectable historical evidence" (that is, written evidence), as to St. Patrick's visit to Lough Derg, yet it would be rash thence to infer that he did not visit it. On the contrary, the presumption in favour of his visit is so well-founded as to fall little short of convincing evidence. In the first place, there is a vivid and continuous tradition, that he visited it for deeds of penance, for retreat and silent prayer; and, seeing that the Irish race had always regarded their patron saint with the most affectionate veneration, and had carefully treasured up, and handed down from generation to generation even minute particulars regarding his life and labours, we should attach great importance to this tradition. Again, Dr. Lanigan records how St. Patrick, being in Tyrconnell, went back eastward towards Lough Erne ; as this course would bring him through the very locality in which Lough Derg is situated, what inconsistency is there in supposing that he then visited it, saw its adaptability for a place of retirement and penitential exercises, and there and then inaugurated it as such ? The allusion in an old office of St. Patrick bears strongly, also, on this point, thus—"*Hic est doctor benevolus, Hibernicorum Apostolus, cui loca purgatoria ostendit Dei gratia,*" *i.e.* that God, by a special favour, pointed out to St. Patrick certain places adapted for penitential exercises, such as Lough Derg certainly is.

Furthermore, the constant devotion to St. Patrick observed at this pilgrimage, the church dedicated to him, his cross, his cave, his bed of hard penance, the name which has been universally assigned to this pilgrimage, viz., St. Patrick's Purgatory, are all so many traditions and proofs in favour of his having hallowed this retreat with his presence, and of having originated those penitential exercises which the pious votaries have ever since so lovingly imitated. And though the narrative of the monk, Henry of Saltrey, contains many exaggerations, his statement with regard to St. Patrick's connexion with this pilgrimage cannot be lightly set aside. Henry lived in the twelfth century, and related what he heard from Gilbert of Lud, and chiefly the wonderful things that happened to Owen, an Irish soldier, who had the courage to enter this cave. Henry of Saltrey says—" The Lord

D

brought St. Patrick into a desert place, and there showed him a round cave, dark within . . . . And since the pilgrim is there purged of his sins, the place is named the Purgatory of St. Patrick."

Also, it may be added, that St. Patrick has been always referred to as the founder of this penitential retreat; now, whenever St. Patrick is referred to simply, and without any additional epithet, it is our national Apostle that is meant; on the other hand, the Abbot Patrick is always called, as if to distinguish him from the Apostle of Ireland, the Abbot Patrick, or Patrick Junior.

The question as to whether the pilgrimage takes its origin from St. Patrick, the Apostle of Ireland, hinges on the previous question. For if, as we hold for certain, our patron saint had visited the place, then it is pretty clear that his spiritual children flocked thither to follow the example of the austerities he there practised, and thus rendered it a place of pilgrimage.

In a rare work, called *Vita Sti. Patricii a Jacobo de Voragine, seu Lombardica Historia* (printed at Nuren - berg, anno 1482), the following is given as the origin of the pilgrimage :—" *Cum beatus Patricius per Hiberniam prædicaret et fructum permodicum faceret, rogavit Dominum ut aliquod signum ostenderet per quod vel territi pœniterent, jussu igitur Dei circulum magnum in quodam loco cum baculo designavit; et ecce terra intra circulum se aperuit, et putens magnus et profundissimus ibidem apparuit. Reve- latumque est beato Patricio quod ibidem quidem purgatorii locus esset, in quem quisquis vellet descendere, alia sibi pœni- tentia non restaret, nec aliud pro peccatis purgatorium*

sentiret. Plerique autem inde non redirent, et quot redirent
eos a mane usque in sequens mane ibidem moram facere
oporteret. Multi igitur ingrediebantur qui de cætero non
revertebant."

That this place was famous as a hermitage and place
of penance long anterior to the time of the Abbot Patrick
is sufficiently clear from this fact alone, that during the
interval the names of two, probably three, of its abbots
are on record, namely, St. Dabheoc, St. Cillene, and St.
Avil. As to St. Dabheoc,* Colgan says that St. Patrick
left him at Lough Derg, in Donegal, in charge of a church,
which in subsequent ages became famous as St. Patrick's
Purgatory. And the Rev. John Francis Shearman of
Howth, in his *Loca Patriciana*, says, "that Colgan's statement about Dabheoc is well-founded ; for when St. Kevin
was at the school of his relative, Bishop Eoghan of
Ardstra, St. Dabhioc, or Bioc, then in extreme old age,
paid frequent visits to this seminary" at Ardstraw, which
he could easily do, owing to the propinquity of his retreat
at Lough Derg. And hence, though the weight of authority forces us to admit that this penitential retreat was
originated by St. Patrick, yet it may be said that his
disciple, St. Dabheoc, by his severe austerities and penances gave great celebrity to this retreat, and added a
great attraction to its pilgrimage. Of him Colgan writes,
"He is called *Dabeocus* in general, and often *Beoanus* in

---

* Dabheoc, when divested of its prefix *do* and *oc*, is the same as
ᚐeoh, or Hugh. In the *Martyrology of Tallagh* the entry is "ᚐeoh,
Lochagerg, *alias* Dabheog."

Latin. He is the patron of a very celebrated church in a certain lake in Ulster, called Loch-Gerg, in which is that celebrated Purgatory of St. Patrick, whence either the lake itself, or the place in which it lies, is called Gleann-Gerc, where in the adjacent territory St. *Dabeocus* is held in the greatest veneration to the present day, and his festivity is observed three days in every year, according to our Festilogies, viz., on the 1st of January, 24th of July, and 16th of December. The *Calendar of Cashel* places his festival day only on the 15th of December. It is related in the beginning of the Irish Life that he had foretold several things about the holiness and virtues of St. Columb many years before the latter was born, from which it follows that he flourished in the time of St. Patrick. He is ranked among the chief saints of Ireland by Cummian."

Colgan traces the pedigree of St. Dabheoc to Dichu, St. Patrick's first convert, from which he infers that he was of the race of the *Dalfiatachs*, and that his country lay about Lecale, in Down. Other authorities trace his lineage and birthplace to Wales.

I am deeply indebted to that learned Irish scholar, Father Shearman, of Howth, for the following genealogical table, with several valuable notes regarding St. Dabheoc, with which he has favoured me. Following the opinion of Colgan, he gives the pedigree of Dabheoc thus—

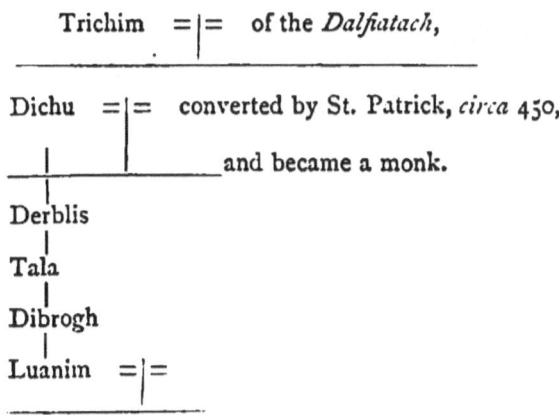

Beoan, or Dabheoc (October 26th or 28th), of Glen Geirg, who flourished about A.D. 610, and is quite different from Dabheoc, or Beoan, son of Brychin, the Cambrian. In the *Naemsencus* leᴀbhᴀⱀ bⱀeᴀc occurs—

> "ⱁᴀbeoᵹ ᵹlⰻⱀⱁⰻ ᵹeⰻⱀᵹ cⱀᴀ
> ⱞᴀc Lцᴀⰻⱀⰻⱞ ⱞц ⱁⰻbⱀoᵹᴀ
> ⱞc Cᴀlᴀ ⱞc ⱁⰻⱀblⰻⱀ ⱀⰻl
> ⱞc ⱁⰻcoⱀ ⱘoⱀ ⱞⱃ Cⱀⰻchⰻⱞ."

In Father O'Hanlon's most learned and invaluable work, *Lives of the Irish Saints* (vol. I., No. 1), the parentage of the Cambrian Dabheoc is thus given:—"St. Dabeog was the son of Brecan, or Bracan, who ruled over a territory in Wales, formerly denominated Brechonia, or Brechinia. The parents of Bracan were his father Bracha, or Bracmeoc, an Irish-born prince, and Marcella, a noble British lady." Father Shearman thinks it must have been the Cambrian Dabeog, who predicted the birth of St. Columba, who was born December 7th, 521. This St.

Dabheoc may have been likewise at Lough Derg, though the 7th century Dabheoc is more likely to be the patron of it. The prediction regarding St. Columba is thus narrated by Father O'Hanlon, in his *Life of St. Dabheoc*, already referred to. He says : " When St. Dabheoc had here " (at Lough Derg, probably), " protracted his vigils to a late hour one night, in company with his clerics, a wonderful brightness appeared towards the northern part of the horizon. The clerics asked their master what it portended. ' In that direction, whence you have seen the brilliant illumination,' said Dabeog, ' the Lord himself, at a future time, shall light a shining lamp, which, by its brightness, must miraculously glorify the Church of Christ. This shall be Columba, the son of Feidlimid, son of Fergus, and whose mother will be Ethnea. For learning he shall be distinguished; in body and soul shall he be chaste ; and he shall possess the gifts of prophecy.' "

Father Shearman adds that " Bioc of *Glen-geirg*, is perhaps, the same as Beon, Bishop of Tamlact McNainn (not identified), and Loċ bṗicτenn (Loughbrickland(?)."

That St. Dabheoc, patron of Lough Derg, came to that lonely island, long known as St. Dabheoc's Island, towards the close of the sixth, or beginning of the seventh century, seems certain. To the austerities practised by this saint, Cummian of Connor refers in a poem on the characteristic virtues of the Irish saints, which is given, with its English version, in the *Martyrology of Tallagh*, edited by the late Rev. Mathew Kelly, D.D., of Maynooth College. The stanza on St. Dabheoc runs thus :—

Mobheog,* the gifted, loved,
According to the synod of the learned,
That often in bowing his head,
He plunged it under water."

Now it is worthy of remark that the aforesaid penitential act for many centuries was practised at this pilgrimage;
and even yet it continues to be observed by some in a
modified way.   Such force, we may well say, has the con-
tinuance of a pious usage in the transmission of historical
facts.

After St. Patrick, St. Dabheoc was the special patron
of this pilgrimage.   There were three festivals annually
observed at Lough Derg in his honour, on the 1st of
January, on the 24th of July, and on the 16th of
December.   These three festivals noted three important
events in his life.   The first may have been his *dies natalis;*
the second the anniversary of his installation as abbot;
and the third his *dies obitus*.   These festivals appear to
have been kept in Colgan's time ; but for many years past
they have not been observed.   At the present day, indeed,
the only one of these festivals which might be observed
is that of the 24th of July, as, during the occurrence of
the others, the station is closed.

We have already seen that the site of the monastery,
founded here by St. Dabheoc, is marked by the old ᴜᵢ𝚛,
which is still discernible on Saints' Island.

The name of St. Dabheoc is perpetuated in the town-

---

* Mobheoc is the same as Dabheoc ; *mo* and *do* being prefixes
denoting affection.

land denomination of Seeavoc (ᚱᚔᚒᚑᚆᚓ ᚅᚐᚁᚆᚓᚑᚌ), which means St. Dabheoc's seat, which stone seat is still to be seen there, much the same as in the days of the saint. The "Seat" lies in an out-of-the-way place, and the way towards it is difficult and precipitous. After sailing from the Ferry-house towards the south-western expansion of the lake, the visitor will perceive a little quay, or landing-place, nearly midway between St. Brigid's Chair and Port-creevy. Taking a direct line from this point straight up the mountain side, he will reach, after proceeding about one hundred perches, a carn-shaped eminence, on the very summit of the mountain. Here a stone seat is certainly to be seen, with a grave-like opening immediately in front of it, measuring about three feet deep, and between four and five feet in length. In this "cave" one could kneel with some difficulty. Its sides were built with stone flags, which, after the lapse of so many centuries, must have slided in, thus leaving the enclosed space at present so confined. It is pretty clear that a covering of some sort must have originally protected this seat and cave from the storms, which, at this elevation, are occasionally somewhat alarming. Sitting on this "Seat" the lake is entirely in the background, and nothing meets the view but a long stretch of mountain, running south towards Pettigoe, and the valley through which ran the ancient roadway to Saints' Island. Standing however in the "cave," and looking towards the north, a full view of Lough Derg meets the eye; and I must confess that a better standpoint could hardly be gained for obtaining a "bird's-eye view" of this most interesting locality.

The best view of the mound, on the summit of which the seat is located, can be obtained as you ascend more than midway from the lake towards it. It is evidently artificial, and was raised by heaping together the heath and sods of the mountain.

At the time this " seat " was constructed, the habitations

St. Dabheoc's Seat.

of the Irish were very rude. Cave-like and beehive shaped edifices (remains of which may still be seen along the western coast of Ireland), were *more patriæ* availed of at this period of transition, having their prototypes in the Pagan period of our country. And hence, the very formation of this "seat," and its archaic character, are the very best evidences of its antiquity, and of its having been really, as in name, used by St. Dabheoc for the two-fold purpose of a seat, or retired place of meditation, and of a cave in which to do penance. At this early period not only the saint's cell was venerated, but also his cross, his bed of penance, and his cave. Thus we learn that amongst other objects connected with St. Kevin in the county of Wicklow, his cave at Glendalough is still traditionally venerated. Here, on this mountain top, the holy Dabheoc detached himself from earthly considerations, and drew nearer to his Creator by the exercise of works of penance and mortification, which indeed were hidden from the eyes of his fellowmen, but recorded in the Register of God.

Nor can we wonder that the saints so loved to fix their haunts among the mountains ; for, are they not the fittest types of fortitude and constancy, power and perseverance? Of old the angels and the ark rested on their summits— the Psalmist wept for Jonathan slain on his own mountains, and he sighed in his soul for the " everlasting hills." They look down unchanged on the changes which take place in everything around them ; and elevate the soul above the passing scene of this world.

St. Dabheoc's Seat gave rise to the denomination See-avoc, the name by which the district in which it lies was anciently known. In after ages the district was divided into sub-denominations—*Portneillinwore* (*i.e.* the harbour of the large island), *Portcreevy* (*i.e.* the bushy harbour), and *Ballymacavany*, the townland in which it is now situated. That these names are of comparatively modern date, probably of the fifteenth or sixteenth century, it is not difficult to guess; whereas the term Seeavoc is probably as old as the days of St. Dabheoc himself.

On Station Island may be seen a fragment of an old stone cross, which is included in the illustration of St. Patrick's Cross given in this work. Mr. Wakeman, to whom is due the credit of being the first who bestowed more than a passing look at this important object, says that it is far older than St. Patrick's Cross, dating as far back as the sixth or seventh century, if we may judge from the style of art displayed on it. This, in all likelihood, is St. Dabheoc's Cross, and was erected over his *aherla*, or grave on Saints' Island. Only the head and arms of this cross remain; the shaft, which must have measured about five feet, having been broken off close by the arms. This shaft is now nowhere to be seen; and I have been informed by the Rev. James M'Kenna, P.P., Brookeborough, a clergyman who has had long and intimate connection with Lough Derg, that he never could make out even a fragment of this shaft anywhere about the lake, though he made diligent search and inquiry after it; the supposition being that it must have been cast into the lake by the iconoclasts, who, during the seventeenth century, razed the structures on Saints' Island.

The measurements of this mutilated cross are—head, one foot; arms, one foot nine inches in length; width of head and arms, six inches; in depth, four inches. At each of the four corners, formed by the shaft and arms of this cross, there is a hollow cutting, like the concave arc of a circle, which is but rarely found on old crosses, and only on those of the earliest date.

The stone of which this cross is formed is schist, which, with mica-slate, is the quality of stone most common in the vicinity of the lake; the supposition being that at this early period, the freestone quarries, which are nine or ten miles distant from the lake, and from which the other inscribed stones, crosses and cut stone at Lough Derg were taken, had not then been discovered.

In the space included between the arms, head and shaft of this cross, there is on both sides of the cross a raised circlet, which is about four inches in diameter. This circle may have been intended to express the catholicity or universality of the Church; but more probably it is a symbolical representation of the Holy Eucharist, which, in the early ages of the faith, owing to the "discipline of the secret," used to be expressed by such symbols. This was the original form of the circle which may now be so commonly seen entwining the arms of our beautiful Celtic crosses.

This mutilated cross was hitherto placed in the centre of one of the saint's "beds" on Station Island, thus showing the sacred character attached to it by the pilgrims, and the care with which it was preserved.

The original site of this ancient cross, which we will designate the cross of St. Dabheoc, was at the saint's grave* within the cemetery on Saints' Island,

---

* In the *Monasticon Hibernicon* (édited by the Most Rev. Dr. Moran), it is said that St. Dabheoc was buried in the abbey, which stood on Saints' Island.

which now presents such deplorable ruin and desolation.

How long St. Dabheoc lived at Lough Derg, or in
what year he died, it has not been ascertained. Taking
it that the two saints of that name, the Cambrian and the
Ultonian, had both lived at Lough Derg, as appears very
probable, it would appear that the Cambrian St. Dabheoc
died during the early part of the sixth century, and before
the birth of St. Columba, which event he predicted. Hence,
if we take, as is commonly supposed, 490 as the year in
which St. Dabheoc arrived at Lough Derg, and 516 or
517 as the year of his demise, we will thus have more
than twenty-five years, during which the saint had pointed
out to the newly-converted Irish nation the bright example
of a penitential life.

Very likely his was one of the eight monastic orders
that were in the early Church in Ireland; for, it is stated
in the life of St. Ciaran of Clonmacnoise, that the order
of St. Molaisre of Devenish was one of the eight orders in
Erin, and that after completing thirty years, Molaisre
went to heaven, A.D. 563. The memory of Molaisre is
venerated on the 12th of September in the Martyrology,
where Ænguis says :—" With the feast of Laisren,* the
beautiful, of multitudinous Devenish." Speaking of St.
Laserian, Sir James Ware says, that he instituted a particular rule, but that his successors took the rule of St.
Augustine. It may have been that St. Molaisre adopted

---

* Molaise, Molaisre, Laisre and Laserian are but different forms
of the same name.

the rule of St. Dabheoc, who was almost his contemporary, and whose monastic house was at that time the most
distinguished in the neighbourhood.

Besides we may reasonably suppose that there continued to exist close intercourse from the very beginning, as if they were branches of the same order, between the religious establishments at Lough Derg and
Devenish. In after ages, when Imar, Archbishop of
Armagh, had introduced the Canons Regular of St.
Augustine to his church and abbey of SS. Peter and Paul,
built about the year 1126, Devenish and Saints' Island,
which had been laid desolate by the Danes, were both re-
peopled by religious of that order. And thus the fellow-
ship which existed from the beginning between these religious foundations, continued on down during the middle
ages.

Nor should I forget to add that one of the penitential
circles, or "beds," on Station Island, round which the pilgrims proceed reciting certain prayers, is the bed of St.
Dabheoc. It is marked on a map of the place, published in Sir James Ware's *Antiquities of Ireland* (London,
1672), and is there called *lectus vel circulus Abogi*, the
latter being a corrupt form for *Dabogi*, or Dabheoc. To
the saint's "cross," "seat," "cave," and "bed," special
veneration appears to have been paid, inasmuch as they
were so intimately connected with the saint's prayer and
penance, and thus they became such a centre of pious
attraction.

As to when the seventh-century St. Dabheoc came to
Lough Derg, or in what year he died, I cannot venture

an opinion. As he seems to have been the special patron of Lough Derg, we may infer that to him were dedicated the seat, the cross, the bed, the island, and the termon-lands. However, owing to the similarity of the names of these two saints, and the want of historical evidence on the point, it is very difficult to draw any definite conclusion thereon.

Despite the absence of written historical evidence, or at best but meagre reference, regarding St. Dabheoc, his memory has been preserved at Lough Derg in the devotion of the pilgrims towards him. His seat, also his cross, his bed of penance, his island, his termon, are all imperishable traditions of his virtues, and of the veneration in which his memory has been held. And thus are preserved, for the edification of remote generations, the lives and actions of those faithful servants of God, who abandoned the world, and, in the solitude of their retreat, devoted themselves wholly to the Divine service, and to the observance of the Evangelical counsels of perfection.

CHAPTER VII.

TERMON-DABHEOC—SUCCESSORS OF ST. DABHEOC—ST.
BRIGID—ANCIENT ROADWAY TO LOUGH DERG.

HE patrimony devoted by our pious ancestors towards the use and support of the
religious foundation on Lough Derg was
known for many ages under the name of
Termon-Dabheoc.   In time this name extended itself to the entire parish, in which
Lough Derg is situated; hence in a list of parishes
of the diocese of Clogher, together with their taxa-
tion, received into the Exchequer in the sixteenth year
of Edward II. (1323), Termondaveog is set down as one
of the churches in the decanate of *Logherny* (*i.e.* Lough
Erne), now the deanery of Enniskillen.   For the last four
centuries, however, these churchlands are called Termon-
Magrath, after the family that became hereditary termoners,
or guardians of this sanctuary and its possessions.

These termonlands are very extensive, and their rental
at the present day is said to reach the sum of £5,000.
The limits of this ecclesiastical property were originally
marked by termon-crosses ; and vestiges of these crosses
and other termon-marks are still discernible.   Relative to
termon-crosses, Dr. Lanigan writes (vol. iv., p. 386) :—
"We find some canons relative to ecclesiastical lands, or
tracts, called *Terminus*, and their boundaries or marks.
'Let the *terminus* of a holy place have marks about it.

Wherever you find the sign of the Cross of Christ, do not do any injury. Three persons consecrate a *terminus* of a holy place, a king, a bishop, and the people.' It appears that crosses might be erected in such holy places, and that this might have been done by either a king, a bishop, or the people."

Though these termonlands did not possess the right of sanctuary, strictly so called, the same as churches and religious houses, yet they were favoured with different immunities and privileges, such as freedom from impost of taxes by the civil authorities, &c.

Of Termon-Dabheoc the following entries are to be found in the *Annals of the Four Masters:*—" A.D. 1196. The son of Blosky O'Currin plundered Termon-Daveog; but in a month afterwards he himself was slain, and his people were dreadfully slaughtered, through the miracles of God and St. Daveog."

" 1345. Nicholas Magrath, coarb of Termon-Daveog, died."

" 1395. Donnell, *i.e.* O'Muldoon of Lurg, was treacherously taken prisoner by the sons of Art Maguire at Termon-Daveog, and delivered up as a captive to O'Donnell."

" 1440. Magrath, Mathew, son of Marcus, coarb of Termon-Daveog, died; and John Boy was elected in his stead."

" 1469. John Boy, the son of John More Magrath, coarb of Termon-Daveog, died; and Dermott, the son of Marcus, son of Maurice Magrath, was made coarb in his place."

" 1496. Con O'Donnell, with the forces of Tyrconnell,

E

Inishowen, and Dartry-Mac'Clancy, turned in pursuit of
Hugh and Maguire, and followed them to Termon-Daveog.
Magrath, *i.e.* Rory, the son of Dermot, son of Marcus,
coarb of that Termon, came to them and warned Con and
the Kinel-Connell not to violate his protection, or the protection of the Termon, by attacking Maguire."

"1562. Magrath, of Termon-Daveog, died."

According to the Rev. John O'Hanlon, in his *Life of
St. Malachy O'Morgair*, the "Coarb was the vicar, a legal
representative of the patron saint, or founder of the
church; but the word *comorbha* is not exclusively ecclesiastical, for in the ancient laws of Erin it meant the heir
or conservator of the inheritance; and it is in the latter
sense it is always used in our ecclesiastical writings.
There was an understood original compact, recognised by
the Brehon laws, which vested the coarbship of the church
and its lands in two families, namely, in that of the
patron saint or founder, and in that of the person who gave
the original site and endowment." From this it is clear
that the Magraths, so long coarbs of this Termon, were
quite distinct from the prior and community of Lough
Derg; and that it was not even necessary, by virtue of
their office, that they should be ecclesiastics.

Whether St. Molaisre of Devenish had lived for any
period at Lough Derg we have no means of finding out.
At any rate it is most probable that he paid frequent
visits to it; and in the supposition that he followed the
rule of St. Dabheoc, and that both houses were sister com-
munities, he may have actually resided for some time at
Lough Derg, for the purpose of following the course of

penance there practised by St. Patrick, and after him by St. Dabheoc. St. Molaisre is yet the titular saint of one of the seven cells or little oratories on Station Island. Two of these cells or " beds " are so closely connected together as to give the appearance of forming but the same " bed." They are known to the pilgrims as the "big bed;" and they are dedicated to SS. Dabheoc and Molaisre, very forcibly suggesting the fraternity and close relationship which existed between these two saints and their respective foundations.

In the southern gable of St. Patrick's church may be seen four inscribed stones, which were previously lying about Station Island, till the Revs. James and John M'Kenna during the summer of 1860 had them carefully placed in their present position. Three of these inscribed stones belong to the last century ; one of them being the date-stone of a little church erected here by Friar Anthony O'Doherty, of the order of St. Francis; the other two having been placed at oratories or " beds " of titular saints of the place. To the fourth inscribed stone, as also an inscription on a corbel-shaped holy-water font still preserved on the island, I shall refer at some length hereafter.

Now one of the inscribed stones referred to goes to show the veneration in which St. Molaisre was held at Lough Derg. The inscription is as follows :—

" I.H.S.
St. Patrick and St. Blosses,*
Pray for us.
P. F. Mc'GRATH."

---

* Blosses is evidently a corrupt form of Molaisre.

It is difficult to say, with any degree of certainty, who was the immediate successor of St. Dabheoc over the community on Saints' Island. Indeed the records regarding Lough Derg for about five centuries after St. Dabheoc are exceedingly meagre ; an entry in the *Annals of the Four Masters*, a few notices in our Martyrologies, with some dim traditions, being almost all we have to aid us (if we except some ancient inscriptions and other objects of archæological interest to which we attach the greatest historical importance) in unravelling the mystery which surrounds Lough Derg during the early centuries of Christian Ireland.

That our early writers have not made frequent and fuller reference to Lough Derg is not to be wondered at ; for it was regarded to some extent as a place of private devotion and penance ; and since this practice was only in keeping with the general spirit and discipline of the early Irish Church, it appeared in no way uncommon or extraordinary, and hence it failed to attract the notice of our annalists and historians, except in a very passing way.

In the *Annals of the Four Masters*, under the year 721, we find reference to another abbot of Lough Derg in the following concise entry :—

" A.D. 721. Cillene of Lough Derg, died."

Now in the *Martyrology of Tallagh* we find no less than thirteen saints of that name mentioned ; some of them having their names merely recorded, others with their dignity, rank and place of residence annexed ; one of the latter, by the way, being no less a dignitary than " Bishop of Tehallen." I consider it extremely probable that St. Cillene, who died at Lough Derg in 721, is the same as St. Cillene recorded in the *Martyrology of Tallagh* under January the 8th, as "Cillene, Abbot."

Another of the inscribed stones in the gable of St. Patrick's Church, commonly called the "Prison Chapel," on Station Island, has the following inscription :—

"I.H.S.
St. Avil, pray for us.
P. F. Mc'GRATH.
Hic fieri fecit.
1753."

I think we may fairly conjecture that St. Avil was abbot on Lough Derg, and one of St. Dabheoc's successors. In the *Martyrology of Tallagh*, under the 22nd of April, we meet with the following entry :—"Abel Mac'Aedha, *potius* Adam."

Now it seems highly probable that this Abel Mac' Hugh and St. Avil designated one and the same individual. Besides, Aedh, or Hugh, is the same name as Dabheoc, when divested of its adjuncts *do* and *oc;* so that in this way the entry in the Martyrology may be taken to mean—Abel Mc'Hugh, *i.e.* Avil the spiritual child, the dear disciple and successor of Hugh, *alias* Dabheoc. St. Avil is still held in veneration at Lough Derg; and to him was dedicated one of the penitential circles, or beds, on Station Island, according to the authority of a little handbook, which for many years past was almost the only guide to the devotional exercises of this pilgrimage; but which was so imperfect and faulty as to excite our wonder that it was not long since superseded.

A St. Fintan would appear to have been numbered among the saints of Lough Derg. One of its islands (which of them we have no means of finding out) had been dedicated to him, and commonly passed under the cognomen of St. Fintan's Island. Whether this was the same as St. Fintan of Clonenagh, we cannot determine. By looking into the festilogies of Irish saints, we find that St. Fintan is a very common name, there being no fewer than seventeen saints of that name recorded in the *Martyrology of Tallagh*. We know that St. Fintan of Clonenagh passed his novitiate under St. Columba, son of Crimthan, who had a school at Tyrdaglass, near Lough Derg on the Shannon. It may have been, indeed, that the similarity in the names of these lakes may have given rise to a mistake. Here at St. Fintan's monastery at Clonenagh were "seven churches," which were first brought under notice by the Rev. John O'Hanlon. At Lough Derg, in Donegal, were also "seven churches," and they are represented at the present day by seven oratories, or penal beds, dedicated to seven of the tutelary saints of the pilgrimage. This mysterious heptarchate of churches appears to have existed at the most notable of the religious foundations in Ireland; and would seem to have been a very favourite institution in our country. Hence we read of the seven churches of Clonmacnoise, of Torry Island, of Glendalough, not to speak of many others.

The late Rev. Dr. Kelly, of Maynooth, the learned annotator of *Cambrensis Eversus*, tells us in his notes to that work :—" As to the stations around the penal beds " (at

Lough Derg), " where little churches formerly stood, the
reader will find much interesting information regarding
analogous institutions in the Bollandists, namely, stations
established by St. Gregory in the basilicas and cemeteries
of Rome, which were frequented in Lent, Rogation days,
and the four great festivals of our Lord."

As to when the number of cells or oratories at Lough
Derg was increased to seven, I cannot say.   It is probable they were not established until after the Augustinian
Canons had taken possession of the place in the twelfth
century; perhaps not, indeed, till the fifteenth or sixteenth
century.   In the *Martyrology of Donegal* (edited by Drs.
Todd and Reeves), we find the following statement, which
has reference to the question under consideration, under
the heading of *Purgatorium Sti. Patricii* :—" There are
five beds of hard penance there, round which the pilgrims
go, the Bed of Patrick, of Columcille, of Brigid, of Adamnan, and of Dabeog.   This is the testimony of Ferghal.
But the b? m! * says that he saw *two* beds there, viz.,
Patrick's and Colum's—48 [hours] without food, without
drink—nine days there altogether.   A pilgrimage during
the day and prayers.   The baking of bread must be
without salt.   Loch-Gerc is its name."

That special devotion was always paid to St. Brigid at
Lough Derg no one can doubt.   Her cross, her bed of
penance, and her chair are lasting mementoes of this devotion.   At the south-eastern corner of St. Patrick's Church
on Station Island, on a large freestone block inserted in

---

* Some writer whose name I have not been able to make out.

the wall, a cross of the Roman model is deeply inscribed. This is known as "St. Brigid's Cross." At what date this cross was cut it is impossible to say; but from its style, and close resemblance to similar inscribed crosses at Clonmacnoise, we may infer that it is a work of the twelfth century, if not of an earlier period. At this cross the pilgrims go through a very solemn and impressive ceremony. After repeating certain prayers on bended knees before it they arise, and, with outstretched arms in front of it, but looking towards the lake, they thrice repeat, "I renounce the devil, the world, and the flesh." One of the seven circles or beds on the island is also dedicated to the "Veiled Nun of Kildare," and is called St. Brigid's Bed.

At the southern shore of the lake, just at the water's edge, a massive detached block of stone will attract the notice of the visitor. Here can be had a good view both of Saints' Island and Station Island, together with the expansive sheet of water of Lower Lough Derg. A more solitary spot, and withal more suggestive of soothing thoughts and devout meditation, could hardly be found. This large stone presents beyond question the outline and appearance of a high-backed chair. The surface of the seat, and also of the back of the chair, is pretty smooth. The seat is slightly concave and reclining backwards. The best view of the "chair" presents itself as you approach within a few oars' distance of it. It is called by the people of the neighbourhood "St. Brigid's Chair" to this day.

In that full and circumstantial account of her life written by Father O'Hanlon, in the second volume of his

Lives of the Irish Saints, we find that St. Brigid visited many of the holy places throughout Ireland. And

St. Brigid's Chair.

though we have no authoritative evidence as to her visit to this locality, on the other hand we have no reason to deny that, attracted by the austere life practised here by St. Dabheoc, she paid a visit to his retreat ; and, after the fatigues of her journey, rested her weary limbs on this stone seat, and from it took a survey of the island hermitage of St. Dabheoc.

As St. Brigid died about the year 520, it must have been during the time the Cambrian St. Dabheoc presided over the religious establishment on Lough Derg, that she visited the place. The place selected by this holy virgin to view this penitential retreat was singularly favourable. The death-like solitude and stillness on all sides, interrupted only by the occasional whir of the moorfowl through the heath on the adjoining mountain, the fitful gust of the breezes over the lake, or the beating of the waves against the "Chair" and along the rocky shore in its vicinity, are calculated to impress on the mind deep and abiding recollections of the "Lake of Penance."

A little to the east of the chair, and bordering on the shore of the lake, may be seen a spa well, largely impregnated with iron. This well is marked on the Ordnance Map of the place.

To the west of St. Brigid's Chair, and about two furlongs from the shore of the lake, but somewhat further from the chair, is situated on the very summit of a mountain a carn-shaped eminence, on the summit of which is St. Dabheoc's Seat, which has been already described in this work.

Writing on Templecarn churchyard we have already seen that the ancient roadway to Lough Derg passed by this old churchyard. And so it did. This ancient road, called by O'Donovan a *via strata*, is given on the Ordnance Survey Map of the place. At the present day it is very difficult to trace the course of this road, owing to the fact that it has been disused for at least between two or three hundred years; during this time heath and bog having accumulated over it where it led through the mountains, and, where it wound its course along the western shore of the lake, the waves having more effectively

destroyed almost every trace of it. Traces of this roadway
may yet be descried over the summit of Portneillinwore hill
(which is convenient to Saints' Island), also in a few places
along the shore of the lake, particularly at Portcreevy
bay, where it quitted the lake and led on through a
mountain valley towards Templecarn and Pettigoe. I
have been told that at certain parts of this roadway,
where the overlying bog has been cut away, large stepping-
stones, arranged in regular order, have been brought to
light, which leaves us to conjecture that these were hollow
parts of the roads that may have been partly flooded.

I have also learned that where this roadway led through
the tortuous defiles of the mountains between Pettigoe and
Portcreevy, the pedestal of an ancient way-side cross may
yet be seen; and that the ground immediately surrounding this pedestal is closely paved with stones which are
worn smooth; the supposition being that the pilgrims here
knelt and offered up a votive prayer either on approaching or quitting the island.

Towards the south-western extremity of Saints' Island
a narrow neck of water separates the island from the mainland; and here, during the time the monastery stood on
Saints' Island, a bridge formed of oaken beams, and rest-
ing on stone piers, connected the island with the mainland.
Of this bridge, Dr. O'Donovan writes in his *Donegal
Letters* :—" The neck of Seeavoc was anciently connected
with Saints' Island by a wooden bridge, supported by stone
pillars, a part of which may yet be seen when the water is
clear. This bridge served the purpose of the present
money-making ferryboat, and was crossed *gratis*." An

embankment of stones extended out into the shallow
water on either side, while a bridge of beams spanned the
deep stream that flows in the centre of this channel, and
that here connects the upper with the lower lake.   Remains of these piers and of the ᴛᴏᴄʜᴀᴘ or causeway leading from them are still to be seen; but of the bridge of
beams there is not a vestige left.

Mr. Wakeman, in his *Antiquities of Devenish*, says that
Devenish was in former times connected with the mainland by a similar ᴛᴏᴄʜᴀᴘ or causeway, some remains of the
stone piers which extended into the water at the eastern
shore of the island, and the place of landing opposite,
being yet apparent.   And the same learned writer says
that some remains of the oaken piles which supported a
bridge of this sort, are still discernible between Inishmacsaint and the mainland.

It is clear, as we have seen, that a paved way or ʙᴏᴛʜᴀᴘ
led in former times across Portneillinwore hill, along the
shore of the lake through Seeavoc, and on to the southern
bay of the lake, called Portcreevy.

After the destruction of the establishment on Saints'
Island in the seventeenth century, and the removal
of the pilgrimage to Station Island, it seems most probable that Portcreevy (*i.e.* the bushy harbour, a name
which it still merits by reason of the number of trees and
bushes to be seen growing there) was used as the place
of embarkation for Station Island.   It would seem that
the modern roadway was soon after established; for, it
not only is the more convenient, direct and shorter route
rom Pettigoe, but also the lake passage from the present

ferryhouse is fully but half the distance as that from Port-creevy to Station Island. On these grounds we may surmise that Portcreevy was not long used as a point of embarkation, and, in consequence, when Portcreevy was given up, the ancient roadway itself became disused.

To return to the point at which I diverted, this ancient roadway, after leaving Portcreevy, proceeded through the rugged defiles of the mountains past Templecarn on to the wooded and fertile banks of Lough Erne. From this road, we may suppose, a branch path turned off to Inishmacsaint; while the main way led on to Devenish, " Devenish of the Assemblies " having been then the chief centre and emporium, so to say, of Fermanagh. Lough Erne having been then and for many ages the highroad and thoroughfare of a great portion of the north-west of Ireland, the monks and pilgrims sailed over its waters by cot or currach towards Devenish, on their destination for the sanctuary of St. Patrick's Purgatory :—

> " With footsteps strong, and bosom brave,
> Looking for that mysterious cave,
> Where the pitying heavens will show
> How my salvation I may gain,
> By bearing in this life the purgatorial pain."*

---

* From Denis Florence MacCarthy's translation of Calderon's *Purgatorio de san Patricio.*

CHAPTER VIII.

ANCIENT INSCRIPTIONS AT LOUGH DERG—LEARNED DIS-
QUISITION OF THE RIGHT REV. DR. GRAVES—THE
ABBOT PATRICK—LEGEND REGARDING THE ABSENCE
OF SALMON FROM ITS WATERS.

N Station Island there are two inscribed stones, which have hitherto been regarded as perfectly undeciperable, and have up to this completely baffled the ingenuity of antiquarian visitors to the place. The first of these inscribed stones is set into the southern gable of St. Patrick's Church. It is a small sand stone, and most probably was the *titulus* of one of the early churches at this pilgrimage. It is very much water-worn, and most of the characters are quite indistinct and illegible. The second inscribed stone is of much more recent date, and is here placed in the same connection with the first, for this reason—that both appear to refer to the same saint. This second inscribed stone is a corbel-shaped holy-water font, which lies on the island.

Being struck with the archaic character of these inscriptions, I requested Mr. Wakeman of Enniskillen to accompany me to the island, in order to have rubbings of these inscriptions taken. This we effected on the 12th of April, 1878. Soon after, Mr. Wakeman sent forward these rubbings to Dr. Graves, Protestant Bishop

of Limerick, who is admittedly one of the foremost
authorities, in the present age, on Ogham and ancient
Irish inscriptions. The result of his Lordship's investigation is nothing short of a most important discovery.
Dr. Graves' learned disquisition on these inscriptions
having been very kindly communicated to me by Mr.
Wakeman, I gladly take the liberty of placing it on record. Dr. Graves writes :—" Being induced by what
you" (Mr. Wakeman) " told me to believe, that the stone
on Station Island, of which you sent me a rubbing,
originally contained the whole of the inscription, I applied
myself to the consideration of it with much care. The
result of my study has been to assure me that I have
substantially made it out, though I may yet find that my
reading requires correction in matters of detail. The
enclosed copy shows you how I deal with it. The
letters and strokes in *red* are what I supplied. I have
taken those in *black* exactly as you represented them.

" Now let us consider the parts of the inscription in
order :—I propose to supply an I at the end of the first
line. Thus, MECI would be the Latinized form of MEIC,
an old, but not the oldest form of the genitive, MAC.

" After the N which commences the second line, I introduce a Y, but with some doubt. In that place I
should rather have expected IS.

"At the end of the same line, I conjecture the diphthong,
Æ. To this I was led mainly by the little stroke going
up obliquely from the top of the vertical stroke, which
your rubbing exhibits. The Λ in the third line has a
square top of this kind.

" At the commencement of the third line, I suggest a Q, which I would read as QU—not an uncommon thing in inscriptions. After SAP, I restore IENT, being perfectly certain that the letters were there once, whether the traces of them remain or not.

Stone built into Wall of Old Chapel, Station Island, Lough Derg.

" In the latter half of the fourth line, I restore PRI, admitting, however, that OPTI may possibly have stood there originally.

" The I at the beginning of your fifth line, I take to

be the last member of an M; and at the end of the
same line I place the word ERAT or FUIT.

"Now as to the meaning of the inscription, I confess
that I entertain some doubt as to the signification of OR.
The inscription plainly being in the Latin language, we
could not expect to find OR DO, or OR AR, because
DO and AR are Irish prepositions, the Latin equivalent
of which would be PRO. It may be that the OR here
is an abbreviation for ORATE PRO; but I cannot
say that I have ever seen an instance of such an abbreviation. It seems to me not improbable that OR is an
abbreviation for ORATORIUM, or ORACULUM.
Both these words are in use to signify a church or
chapel. The former occurs repeatedly with that meaning in Adamnan's Life of St. Columbkille. As to the
name which follows, it seems to me that it can be
nothing else than MACNISSE.

"This was the name of a very famous man, a contemporary of St. Patrick and Bishop of Connor; and it is a
matronymic, for he was called after his mother, CNESS.
That would account for the termination Æ in the Latinized form of the name. You will find the whole history
of this eminent saint and bishop in Dr. Reeves' *Ecclesiastical Antiquities of Down, Connor, and Dromore* (pp.
237-9); and take note especially of the fact that he was
a great traveller—in fact a pilgrim—in consequence of the
sin which he had committed. Having visited both Rome
and Jerusalem, he might thus have acquired the reputation
of being eminently *sapiens*. He died in the year 514. I
do not suppose that the inscription is so old as that, but I

F

regard it as being very ancient.   As you say in your letter,
it must be very ancient, or comparatively modern.   If it
was of the eighth, ninth, tenth, or eleventh century, we
should almost certainly have the rounded forms of the
letters E, M, N, T, U ; and the O, instead of being large,
would be rather smaller than the other capitals.   The M "
(the extremities of the vertical lines of this letter are connected by two lines drawn transversely) " seems to be an
ornamental initial.

"This MACNISSE had another name.   He was called
CAEMAN BREAC, the Latinized form of which is
CAEVANUS.   Now if you look at the passage in the Tripartite Life of St. Patrick, to which Dr. Reeves refers, you
will find a very sad and strange story about this man's *hand*.

"Is it not possible that the other inscription, of which you
sent me a rubbing, is to be read MANUS COIVANI?

" This whole matter is so curious, that it deserves the
most careful investigation.   For my part, I should not
like to publish the views which I have stated in this letter
until I had seen carefully made paper-moulds of the two
inscriptions, if only that they might enable me to pro-
nounce a positive opinion as to the mode in which the
inscriptions should be read, and the age of the writing."

Acting on Dr. Graves' suggestion, and at my request,
Mr. Wakeman paid an additional visit to Station Island
on the 23rd of May, when he made fresh and very perfect
rubbings of the two inscriptions, as well as two casts in
paper.   These rubbings and paper-moulds brought out the
very important fact that all the letters in the inscription,
supplied or suggested by Dr. Graves, are to be found

on the stone. The last word in the inscription is FUIT.

Now, as to the person referred to in this inscription, there are two saints of that name referred to in our early ecclesiastical records. One of these is thus mentioned in the *Four Masters:* "A.D. 589. St. Mac Nisse, Abbot of Cluain-Mic-Nois for a period of sixteen years, died on the tenth of the month of June." In the Annals of Clonmacnoise it is thus entered:—"A.D. 587. Mac Nissi, an Ulsterman, third Abbot of Clonvicnose, died in the sixteenth year of his place." Having been from Ulster, he may have gone on pilgrimage to Lough Derg—where he died and was buried on Saints' Island—and in course of time a church with this inscription was erected to his memory. This opinion, however, is hardly probable, as we have no evidence to sustain it.

The Mac Nisse referred to in the inscription appears to be St. Mac Nisse, first Bishop of Connor, and Abbot there.

The Bollandists' *Acta Sanctorum* at the 3rd of September, give the Acts of St. Aengus Mac Nisse. He was baptized by St. Patrick, and was educated by St. Olcan, or Bolcan, to whose possessions he succeeded. He founded the monastery of Connor; visited Rome and Jerusalem as pilgrim; predicted the birth of St. Comgall, founder of Bangor; enjoyed the friendship of St. Brigid; and trained to a life of sanctity St. Colman, first Bishop of Dromore. He died September 3rd, 514. He is entered in the "Feilire" of St. Aengus as—

mac nisse co milid
o Chonderid maraid;

which is rendered in English :—

> Mac Nisse with thousands
> From the great Condere."

He is called in a gloss on the " Feilire," caeman bpeac mac niri.

Now it is likely that St. Mac Nisse, through penance for his sins, went on pilgrimage to St. Patrick's Purgatory on Lough Derg, and that the inscribed stone already referred to was erected in the oratory in which he performed such severe penance ; or that a memorial church, of which this was the *titulus*, was soon after erected there. The admitted antiquity of the inscription, which belongs to the sixth or seventh century at latest, confirms this conjecture. But this opinion is greatly strengthened by the second inscription, or legend, which appears on a corbel-shaped font, which now lies on Station Island. This legend reads :—

In the second line of this inscription a small v is inserted after the first I, which shows that the engraver had forgotten it till after the remainder of the inscription was made out, and then inserted it in its present crushed-up position.

This inscription Dr. O'Donovan saw on his visit to Lough Derg, and though he looked upon it as comparatively modern, he could not understand it. His conjecture was that it referred to one of the Coarbs of Termon-Dabheoc.

Cæman Breac was a cognomen bestowed on St. Mac Nisse, and had its origin in the following melancholy story, taken from Colgan's "Trias Thaumaturga" (Septima Vita S. Patricii, Lib. ii., cap. 134, p. 147) :—"*Patricio in iisdem partibus* (Scil Rathmugid, now Armoy, Co. Antrim) *agenti contigit alius, non minus miserandus sed et magis pudendus casus. Mac-Nessius enim postea Antistes Connorensis, dum in pietate et bonis disciplinis apud Patricium educaretur, Magistro inscio implicavit se primo incautis, ac paulatim suspectis alterius sexus consortiis, lapsu cum ipsius S. Antistitis sorore vel nepte insimulatus fuerit se faede maculasse. Lapsus ille ad aures Patricii perlatus ita sanctissimum exacerbavit Magistrum, ejusque animum, iramque vindicem contra discipulum exacuit, ut illico precatus et severe imprecatus sit manum illam, quae membrum illud vivum et summae spei, a reliquo sancto sui sodalitii corpore, suis actibus fœdisque contractibus segregavit, in tanti scandali publicam vindictam, cœtero corpore abscissam iri. Et ecce res mira ! manus Macnessii extemplo abscissa in terram cadit, et in perpetuam rei mirabilis, justæque vindictæ memoriam, in loco quid einde Carn-lamha, i.e. tumulus manus, appellatus, tumulatus reconditur. Macnessius vero lapsu sanctior vitam, quam turpi illa nota sic fœde maculavit, egregia mox pœnitentia*

*restauravit, multisque postea signis et virtutibus testatissimœ
sanctitatis mirabilem reddidit et sanctissime finivit."*

From these inscriptions we may justly infer that the
pilgrimage of Lough Derg is of very early origin, that St.
Mac Nisse, the contemporary of St. Patrick, was very
probably on pilgrimage there, and that therefore the pilgrimage must have been originated by St. Patrick himself.

In the ninth century there was a person named the
Abbot Patrick connected with Lough Derg. It appears
he was superior of the religious establishment there for
some time, and afterwards became Abbot of the principal
house of his order at Armagh. His feast is commemo-
rated on the 24th of August, and his name is entered in
the *Martyrology of Tallagh* as "Patrick hostiarius et Abbas
Armacanus." He is said to have written a life of our
national Apostle; and was considered by some, how
erroneously we have seen, to have been the founder of the
"Purgatory," or place of penance at Lough Derg. His
death is supposed to have occurred about the year 850.

Regarding him, or St. Patrick *major* (it is not stated
which), a singular tradition is preserved at Lough Derg,
which obtains implicit credence amongst the artless and
simple-minded inhabitants of that neighbourhood.

Now, as to the traditions here referred to, though I do
not profess myself so incredulous in the matter of local
traditions as Dr. O'Donovan professes himself, yet I well
know that the historical accuracy of many of them cannot
be sustained; nor in relating them do I undertake to
establish their accuracy, merely stating them as I received

them, and leaving it to the readers to attach to them whatever importance they may deem fit.

Since the Celtic race has been always a highly imaginative race, we need not wonder that some historical facts, and especially certain events in the lives of the Irish saints, who were so affectionately venerated, became surrounded and embellished by poetic and imaginary glosses, till in the lapse of time the nucleus of fact became so entangled in the network of fiction as to be hardly distinguishable from it. And hence it comes that many of the popular traditions of our country are to be received with considerable caution and reservation.

But though some of these traditions may not be relied on as conveying historical truth, yet they are valuable in a variety of ways, and therefore worthy of preservation.

Many of these traditions contain a *grain* of historical truth, and when viewed in the light and with the aid of contemporaneous events, are found of much advantage to the historian; while such as are purely imaginary and legendary are also useful, inasmuch as they suggest what were the manners and customs, the simple and confiding faith, the social habits, the modes of thought, &c., of our remote ancestors.

To return to my subject. The story is told that in ancient times Lough Derg abounded in salmon and salmon-trout, just the same as its next neighbour, Lough Erne. The fishful lake gave an unfailing supply to the frugal table of the good monks, and little were the exertions needed in having always at hand a plentiful supply of this delicious and highly-prized fish. On a certain occasion the monks were expecting St. Patrick on his visitation, and had been out fishing all day, in order to have some salmon for the saint's repast. However, they failed in catching any, and were sorely perplexed to find their hospitality thus put to so cruel a test ; which, when the saint had heard, he foretold that salmon would no more inhabit the waters of Lough Derg. And, as if to corroborate the truth of the foregoing incident, the legend goes on to say that about-sixty years ago a gentleman of the sceptical school, having heard the story as already narrated, put himself to great extremes in order to falsify the saint's prediction. He had salmon conveyed from a distance, carefully marked and deposited in the lake ; when lo ! the very next morning the salmon were found in a net, which was placed in the River Derg to prevent their escape.

Little over forty years ago Dr. O'Donovan related the self-same legend ; and, if it be only to show how much these legends are altered and exaggerated, even in a short period of time, I shall give his version of it. He says : " No salmon come into the lake, though they come up to the very throat of the river. Two fishermen (who had a weir near the source of the Derg) cast two live salmon into the lake not many years ago, to see if they'd remain there ; and in order to know them they cut off a part of their fins and tails, but, on their return, they found the same salmon caught in their cochall, or net. This is attributed to the curse of St. Patrick."

As a matter of fact, salmon cannot be found in Lough Derg. The lake, however, abounds in trout, and affords

excellent fishing. In this respect perhaps no other lake
in Ireland can compete with it. During the summer and
autumn a day seldom passes without witnessing a number
of arrivals of those bent on this fine Waltonian sport;
and the followers of the angle are generally rewarded with
a numerous "take." Trout weighing six or eight pounds
are occasionally hauled in; but the class most commonly
caught do not exceed a pound in weight. When a gentle
"fresh" is blowing, no more contemplative or enticing
pastime could be desired than playing a well-trimmed
"cast" off the shoals and reefs, which are so numerous
throughout the lake. And we can well imagine how the
monks of Lough Derg in the olden time, albeit their
prayerful and penitential lives, enjoyed "to their hearts'
content" this delightful recreation, as they sailed over its
waters in their skin-covered currachs.

Eels, also, are to be found in Lough Derg. Near the
mouth of the River Derg remains of an eel-weir may be
noticed.

Of late years pike has found its way into the lake, some
large fish of this class having been caught weighing over
thirty pounds. These "fresh-water sharks" up to this
have made sad havoc on the trout of the lake, but it is
satisfactory to find that large numbers of them, during the
spawning season each year, are netted in the streams flowing into the lake, and in this way, it is hoped, they will
be diminished. Through the surrounding mountains, foxes
have been a similar source of destruction to hares and
heathfowl; their number, however, is very much reduced,
as each year beyond a score of them are caught in traps.

On the northern shore of the lake, near where the River
Derg debouches, may be seen a beautiful white strand.
Smoothly-rounded pebbles, small shells and crustacea,
such as may be seen on the sea-shore, are here to be met
with.   That many of the lakes and rivers of Ireland contain pearls, is beyond question ; of this the Rivers Bann
and Strule are notable instances.   That Lough Derg also
produces pearls, has been lately ascertained.   In the
summer of 1874, a pearl-fisher came to the lake on pilgrimage.   He was an Italian, and, like his countrymen,
possessed the gift of music in a high degree.   It is said of
him at Lough Derg, that in his journey through these
mountains he wakened up many sweet echoes by his
music.   Having reached the lake, he made a search for
pearls along the shore ; and was successful in collecting
some of these rare gems, which, being small and of rather
inferior quality, were worth, as he said, but a few shillings
each.

CHAPTER IX.

DESTRUCTION OF THE MONASTERY OF ST. DABHEOC BY THE DANES—ITS COLONIZATION BY AUGUSTINIAN CANONS— PILGRIMAGE OF THE KNIGHT OWEN.

> "He next for Ireland shaped his course,
> And saw the fabulous Hibernia, where
> The goodly sainted elder made the cave,
> In which men cleansed of all offences are ;
> Such mercy there, it seems, is found to save."—
> Ariosto, *Orlando Furioso*, translated by W. S. Rose.

ROM the fifth till the close of the eighth century, Ireland won for herself that glorious distinction among the nations of being called the *Insula Doctorum et Sanctorum.* From the beginning of the ninth century, however, down to the battle of Clontarf in 1014, the scene changed. During this period the Danes plundered and laid desolate very many of the religious houses throughout Ireland. That Lough Derg shared in the common ruin, is only too likely ; for, we find in the *Four Masters*, under the year 836, that " the churches of Lough Erne were destroyed by the Galls" (the Danish invaders), "with Clones, Devenish, &c." During the long and cruel wars with the Danes, who are called in our annals " foreigners," and also " black Gentiles," pilgrimage to the shrine of St. Patrick's

Purgatory, even supposing that the place had escaped their notice, would be certainly a most perilous undertaking. And hence we may at least infer that this sanctuary, if not altogether destroyed, had been almost completely abandoned during a considerable interval, and had lost in the meantime much of its former lustre.

Some time after the Danes were expelled, religious of the Augustinian Order were introduced into Ireland. They took possession of the ruined cloisters of Lough Derg, Devenish, Clones, and many others throughout Ireland. Imar, Archbishop of Armagh, is, indeed, said to have been the first to introduce them into Ireland, about the year 1126, and to have put under their charge the abbey founded by him at Armagh, and placed under the invocation of the Apostles SS. Peter and Paul. It is asserted that the monastery erected by these venerable canons at Lough Derg was also dedicated to the same holy Apostles. Ware states that this house of the Augustinian Canons at Lough Derg, according to the Register of John Bole (some time Archbishop of Armagh, and who died A.D. 1470), is called "the filial place of the monastery of the Apostles Peter and Paul of Armagh."

And so widespread did this order become throughout Ireland, that, at the time of the suppression and confiscation of their houses and property in the sixteenth century, no less than two hundred and thirty-one houses belonged to this order.

With the introduction of the Canons Regular the second epoch in the history of Lough Derg is reached, which so far excelled the glory of the first, as the third epoch, dating from the Reformation, is destined, we hope, to transcend the glory of both. Under the pious canons life was again infused into the withered bones, pilgrimage to Lough Derg received a fresh impetus, and its sanctuary soon re-appeared in still greater proportions and beauty. The Canons Regular appear to have tenanted Saints' Island for about four hundred years, from the twelfth till the sixteenth century.

Dr. Lanigan, in his *Ecclesiastical History of Ireland* (vol. i., p. 368), exhibiting a want of taste and judgment so little in keeping with his acknowledged character as an historian, writes :—" It will not be expected that I should waste my time with giving an account of the so-called Patrick's Purgatory of Lough Derg, or examining if there could be any foundation for attributing it to our Apostle. It is never mentioned in any of the lives, nor was it, I believe, heard of until the eleventh century, the period at which the Canons Regular at first appeared. For it was to persons of that order, as the story goes, that St. Patrick confided the care of that cavern of wonders." It is easy to understand how Dr. Lanigan has been led into this mistake, when we consider that he spent so many years of his life out of Ireland ; and, though he was profoundly conversant with the historical writings and records of his country, yet its archæology, topography, and local tradi-tions—such fruitful sources of history—were to him a sealed fountain. Besides, if only such facts as are related in the early Lives and Acts of St. Patrick were to be ad-mitted, then we should reject as spurious very many state-ments and traditions, not only as regards St. Patrick, but

the other Irish saints in general, which are accepted by
historians as established facts.   Strange to say, Dr. Lanigan seems to base his argument against the origin and
antiquity of St. Patrick's Purgatory on the authority of a
little tract, which Colgan says he found in a MS. placed
after the end of the *Vita Tripartita*, and which he attri-
butes to the author of the Tripartite Life.   That it was
not written by the author of the Tripartite seems certain,
from the mention in it of Canons Regular, a class of persons then unknown.   It appears to be a transcript of the
narrative of the monk, Henry of Saltrey.   In this little
tract it is said :—"*Statimque Beatus Patricius in eodem
loco ecclesiam construxit, et Beati Patris Augustini Canoni-
cos vitam apostolicam sectantes in ea constituit; fossam autem
praedictam quae in caemeterio est extra frontem ecclesiae
orientalem, muro circumdedit, et januas serasque apposuit,
ne quis eam ausu temerario et sine licentia ingredi praesu-
meret, clavem vero custodiendam commendavit Priori ecclesiae ejusdem, et quoniam homo a peccatis purgetur, locus
ille Purgatorium Sti. Patricii nominatur.*"

As the Canons Regular re-peopled most of the monasteries laid desolate during the Danish wars, the custom
gradually obtained of calling their monastic predecessors
Canons Regular, and in this way St. Patrick himself was
called a Canon Regular, and his feast regularly observed
in their order.

Had Dr. Lanigan and the Spanish critic Feijoo (the
latter of whom seemed to think that the visions related of
the mediæval pilgrims constituted the origin of the pilgrimage) only thought of this—had they but known the

ancient remains, inscriptions, traces, traditions at the place, as well as references in the ancient Irish writings pointing to St. Patrick, St. Dabheoc, and other holy abbots who presided over the monastery of Lough Derg, they would have been spared the opprobrium of assailing this venerable pilgrimage, which is one of the most precious legacies bequeathed by St. Patrick to the Irish race.

Jocelyn also impugns the Patrician origin of Lough Derg, for the sole reason, as it would appear, that it detracts from the fame of his favourite pilgrimage on Croagh-Patrick, that of Lough Derg having been established, as he says, by the Augustinians in opposition to it. But the reasons we have adduced against Dr. Lanigan's view will also sufficiently explain Jocelyn's objection.

Touching the occupation of Lough Derg by the Augustinians, the following lengthy extract, from Dr. Lanigan's *Ecclesiastical History of Ireland* (vol. iv., p. 348), will be interesting :—

"About the twelfth century the Irish monasteries very generally adopted the rule of the Canons Regular of St. Augustine. Nor was the transition difficult : for the old Irish rules did not, in substance, differ much from that of the said canons, inasmuch as they were not as strictly monastical as those of the Egyptian, Basilian, or Benedictine monks, and allowed, without particular dispensation, the union of the active service of the Church, such as practised by the secular clergy, with the monastic regulations, which, although varying more or less, were, as I have often remarked, founded on the system which St. Patrick had seen followed at Lerins and at Tours, and which he introduced into Ireland. Now the characteristic feature of the Canons Regular, which distinguishes them from monks, emphatically so called, is, that although they make vows and are bound to observe certain laws similar to those of the monks, they are capable of practising the functions which usually belong to the secular clergy. Yet the system of the ancient Irish clergy was much more severe than the Canons regular, as is clear from the rule of St. Columbanus, which was taken from those of the monasteries in Ireland, particularly that of Bangor, of which that great saint had been a member."

From this we can understand how certain of the Priors of this monastery, and, doubtless, others of the community as well, are recorded as holding parishes and other dignities in the diocese within which this establishment was situated.

Some time after the Canons Regular had come to reside at Lough Derg, there occurred an event which tended to give the Purgatory much of its Continental fame. It so happened in the twelfth century, that an Irish soldier, named Owen, who had served under the standard of King Stephen, and who had been a crusader, on returning home after long service, felt remorse of conscience for his sins ; and so he resolved on making a pilgrimage to St. Patrick's Purgatory, there to find rest for his troubled soul. This narrative regarding the Knight Owen is to be received with great limitation ; for it was written at a time when, owing to the crusades, the troubadours had brought home from the East sensational, romantic and exaggerated accounts of the deeds of chivalry of the Christian Knights. This taste for the sensational had pervaded the literature of the age ; and hence the narrative of Henry of Saltrey, the poems founded on it by Dante, Ariosto and Calderon, must be considered as containing much that is purely poetic and imaginary. Owen, having obtained the usual permission from the Prior of the island, as well as from the Bishop of the diocese, both of whom strove to dissuade him from his purpose, prepared himself by a fifteen days' fast and prayer to enter the cave. After this, Mass was said, the pilgrim received Holy Communion, a salutary instruction was given, and a procession of the monks was formed, in order to conduct the pilgrim to the mouth of the cave, as it is thus related in the metrical version :—

> " Every priest and every man
> Went with hym yn processoun ;
> And as lowde as they myghte crye,
> For hym they songe the letanye."

The Prior having secured the door of the cave, the knight soon found himself in a large cloistered hall, in which were fifteen religious, clothed in white garments. One of them, preparing him for the attacks of the evil spirits he was to encounter, warned him to invoke the powerful name of Jesus to his aid. This advice is thus given in the same metrical version of Saltrey's narrative :—

> " But if they will thee beat or bind,
> Look thou have these words in mind :
> ' Jesus, as thou art full of might,
> Have mercy on me, sinful knight !'
> And evermore have in thy thought
> Jesus, that thee so dear has bought."

On being left alone, the pilgrim Owen was attacked by the evil spirits, and was preserved from the fiery punishments prepared for him by uttering the prayer, " Jesus, as thou art," &c. In this cave he saw souls undergoing the most terrible torments. From the vision of hell and pur-

G

gatory the knight was led to a gate in a resplendent wall, which was set with pearls and precious stones. This heavenly sight caused him to forget the dangers and sufferings he had hitherto undergone. Here the most enchanting sights and the sweetest melody captivated his heart, so that he desired never to depart from this paradise. But he was not permitted to remain there ; and on his return met with the fifteen ecclesiastics he had seen when first he entered the cave. Having spent a day in their society, and being made acquainted by them with the future events of his life, he left the cave, and received the congratulations of the Prior and canons on his safe return. Having spent fifteen more days on the island, and after relating his vision and adventures to the community of monks, he took his departure from Lough Derg, and amongst others communicated the account of his pilgrimage to Gilbert of Lud, an English monk, who, in his turn, related it to Henry of Saltrey. After leading a truly Christian life to a ripe old age, death closed the pilgrim-soldier's career—

> " He died and went the bright way,
>   To the bliss that lasts for aye ;
>   To that bliss may He us bring
>   That of all is Lord and King."

Henry of Saltrey thus accounts for his knowledge of Owen's vision :—He says that Gervasius, Abbot of Louth, in Lincolnshire, obtained from King Stephen a grant of land in Ireland on which to build a monastery. For this purpose one of his monks, Gilbert, was sent into Ireland with the Knight Owen, who accompanied him as servant and interpreter of the Irish language. Whenever they were alone together the monk asked him minutely concerning Purgatory, and the marvellous modes of punishment which he had there seen and felt; but the knight, who could never hear about Purgatory without weeping bitterly, told his friend, for his edification, and under the seal of secrecy, all that he had seen and experienced, and affirmed that he had seen it all with his own eyes. By the care and diligence of the monk all that the knight had said was reduced to writing, together with the narratives of the bishops and other ecclesiastics of that country, who, for truth's sake, gave their testimony to the facts. Lately, also, I did speak with one who was nephew of Patrick,* the third of that name, the companion of St. Malachius, by name Florentianus, in whose bishopric, as he said, that Purgatory was; of whom having curiously inquired, he answered: "Truly, brother, that place is within my bishopric, and many perish in that Purgatory; and those, who by chance return, do, by reason of the extreme torments they have endured, ever look pale and languid." The aforesaid narrative the said Gilbert did often repeat in my hearing, according as he had often heard it from the knight.

Henry of Saltrey wrote his account of Owen's pilgrimage in Latin prose, in the year 1153. The narrative was translated into several languages in the metrical style then so popular. According to Sister Mary F. Clare, in her

---

* No such name is to be found in Ware's List of Bishops for Clogher or Raphoe about the time in question.

Life of St. Patrick, there are some of these metrical ver-
sions still in existence.   There are two of them in the
British Museum.   One is contained in the Cotton collection, and dates from the fifteenth century ; the other is a
MS. of the fourteenth century in the Auchinleck collection in Scotland.   In the same valuable work of the "Nun
of Kenmare" is given a vignette representing a pilgrim
entering the purgatorial cave, followed by a procession of
monks chanting hymns.

With regard to the penance performed by the Knight
Owen, there is no reason for saying that it differed substantially from the course of penance there pursued at
the present day, highly embellished though the statement
be by the chronicler as well as the pilgrim.   It is even
quite possible that visions regarding the future state of
the soul—regarding the different degrees of punishment
for sin—and also the happy state of the blessed, may
have been vouchsafed to this great penitent—such visions
God having deigned to grant to many of the saints—
among others to His illustrious servants, St. Catherine
and St. Theresa.

At all events, the narrative of the Knight Owen served,
under divine Providence, to spread abroad the fame of
St. Patrick's Purgatory, and to attract to its sanctuary,
from every nation throughout Christendom, pilgrims of
every rank, from the prince to the peasant.

Henry of Saltrey's narrative had been copied from
monastery to monastery, till it became quite familiar
over the continent of Europe.   It had also found its
way into the hands of the great mediæval poets.   Ariosto

had read it, as appears from the extract prefixed to this chapter. It would also appear from the plan and various passages in the *Divina Comedia*, that "the divine poet, the inimitable Dante," had been conversant with it. It is stated that the second part of the *Divina Comedia*, "Il Purgatorio," is founded on Saltrey's account of Lough Derg. The Spanish poet, Calderon—so celebrated for his sacred dramas—upon this same pilgrimage, wrote one of his most charming plays, to which we have already referred, and shall have occasion to refer again hereafter.

CHAPTER X.

TIERNAN O'ROURKE, PRINCE OF BREFFNY, ON PILGRIMAGE AT LOUGH DERG—DISTINGUISHED FOREIGN PILGRIMS— NARRATIVE OF JACOBUS DE VORAGINE.

TIERNAN O'ROURKE, prince of Breffny, was one of the most warlike of Irish chieftains. For about half a century, from 1124 down to the year 1172, when he met with an untimely death, he took part in the wars, predatory incursions, deeds of daring and bloodshed, which distracted his unhappy country, as also in the laudable attempt to resist the English invasion. In 1152, his wife, Dervorgilla, that "degenerate daughter of Erin," eloped with his rival, the infamous M'Murrough. Dervorgil, after having reached the advanced age of eighty-five, closed her ill-fated career in the convent of Mellifont in the year 1193, after undergoing a lengthened course of penance.

It is stated that at the time of her elopement with M'Murrough, her husband had been away on pilgrimage; and the tradition is kept at Lough Derg that it was there he sought consolation for his troubled conscience when he returned to find himself betrayed by M'Murrough. Dr. O'Donovan, in his *Donegal Letters*, also refers to the same tradition. This incident is wedded to immortal verse in the well-known melody of Moore, beginning thus :—

> " The valley lay smiling before me,
>   Where lately I left her behind ;
>   Yet I trembled, and something hung o'er me,
>   That sadden'd the joy of my mind.
>   I looked for the lamp which, she told me,
>   Should shine when her pilgrim return'd,
>   But though darkness began to infold me,
>   No lamp from the battlements burn'd."

Nor will it militate against this tradition to say that on the occasion referred to, Tiernan O'Rourke made pilgrimage to Clonmacnoise, or some other of the many places of pilgrimage which were then frequented throughout Ireland; for about this period it was quite usual to make pilgrimage, without interruption, round the most famous sanctuaries of Ireland. Even those who journeyed to foreign sanctuaries, fortified and prepared themselves for such distant journeys by first making pilgrimage to the most famous shrines of religion in their own country. To this effect different instances are recorded in the registries of Armagh ; and a remarkable instance is there related of one Æneas M'Michæl, who, by way of penance, visited no less than seventeen places of pilgrimage throughout Ireland, among the rest "St. Patrick's Purgatory at Lough Derg, in O'Donnell's country."

The Rev. Mervyn Archdall, of the Fermanagh family of that name, and who wrote his *Monasticon Hibernicon*, about the middle of the last century, mentions a few facts regarding St. Patrick's Purgatory, during the time the Augustinians were in charge of it, which I have not seen stated elsewhere.

Archdall writes :—"St. Dabheoc is said to have been buried in this abbey" (on Saints' Island). "It had a fine chapel, with convenient houses for the monks, the remains of which may yet be seen. One of the St. Patricks was Prior here about the year 850.

" Notwithstanding the reputed holiness of this celebrated monastery, it was plundered and reduced to ashes by Bratachus O'Boyle and MacMahon, A.D. 1207. John was Prior in 1353."

The history of Lough Derg during the thirteenth, fourteenth, and fifteenth centuries, is to be chiefly found in the accounts written of it by distinguished foreigners, who braved the dangers of a journey, then so fraught with peril, in order to pass through the penitential exercises of this celebrated sanctuary. Besides the history of St. Patrick's Purgatory, printed in the works of Mathew Paris, the author of which was Henry, Monk of Saltrey, in Huntingdonshire, and who lived about the middle of

the twelfth century, there are several other manuscript
accounts extant in different libraries.   One of these is to
be found among the Barberini MSS., and is called *Purgatorium S. Patricii, narrante Gilberto Monacho Ludensi,
post abbate de Basingewereck in Anglia.*   Another, in the
same collection, is called *Visio ejusdem Fratris conversi
in Anglia, quam habuit circa annum* 1196.

Another MS. in the Cottonian collection is called,
*Opusculum de quadam visione terribili de suppliciis ani-
marum post obitum corporis: facta Edmundo, Monacho
de Eynesham, regnante R. Ricardo.*

In the year 1358, Edward III. gave testimonials to
Malatesta, a nobleman from Hungary, and Nicholas de
Biccariis of Lombardy, to certify their descent into the
cave of St. Patrick's Purgatory.   In the year 1365, the
Prior of Lough Derg received a letter, asking him to give
a kind reception to two distinguished foreign pilgrims,
John Bonham and Guido Cessy.   John Garry and Francis
Proty, priests of Lyons, and John Burgess, applied for
leave to go to the Purgatory, "sanctified by the forty
days' fast and prayer of St. Patrick."   In the year 1409,
Sir William Staunton descended to the cave.   He wrote
an account of his pilgrimage, which runs through several
hundred pages.   It is entitled, "Here begynneth ye
revelacon ye which William Staunton saw in Patrick's
Purgatorie, the Friday next after ye feast of ye exalta-
tion of the Crosse in the year of our Lord MCCCCIX."
Another account of this pilgrimage was written about
this period by a Knight of Hungary.   It is named,
Præmium Memoriale super visitatione Domini Laurentii

Ratholdi militis et baronis Hungariæ factum de Purgatorio S. Patricii in insula Hiberniæ. Froissart gives an account of Sir W. Lysle's and another knight's visit to the cave, when Richard was in England.

In the Bodleian Library is preserved a MS., called *Tractatus brevis, sed imperfectus de S. Patricii Purgatorio.* In the same place a MS., entitled *Narratio de pœnis Infernalibus,* in which there is mention of St. Patrick's Purgatory. In the library of Trinity College, Dublin, there is a MS. styled *Vita Sancti Patricii Episcopi et Confessoris; item de Purgatorio Hiberniæ.* There is also a MS. in the Vatican Library, by Peter Lombard, Primate of Ireland, which is designated *Relatio de Purgatorio Sancti Patricii in Hibernia.*

Besides these there are many other manuscripts treating of St. Patrick's Purgatory, which are still extant in some of the principal libraries throughout Europe, which fact of itself clearly shows how widespread was the fame of this pilgrimage during the middle ages, and what a firm hold it had taken on the religious sympathies of that period.

In a work of the fifteenth century, written by Jacobus de Voragine, and printed at Nuremberg in the year 1482, under the title of *Legenda Aurea,* is recorded an account of a vision with which a certain pilgrim, named Nicholas, was favoured at St. Patrick's Purgatory. So closely does this narrative resemble that of Henry of Saltrey, that we might almost suppose it to have been borrowed from that writer. Of this narrative, which is written in Latin, I here insert the English version, not so much because I attach much historical importance to it, but principally as an instance of the religious tales of the period.

Jacobus de Voragine writes :—" A long time, therefore, after the death of St. Patrick, a nobleman, named Nicholas, who had been guilty of a great many sins, being smote with contrition, wished to undertake a pilgrimage to St. Patrick's Purgatory. Having endured, as was the custom, various acts of mortification during the space of fifteen days, on the door having been opened by a key which was kept in the abbey, he descended into the above-named cave, on the side of which he observed a doorway. Entering by this way he found there an oratory, into which some monks, clothed in white, and repeating the office, had entered, and forewarned Nicholas that he had many temptations of the devil to encounter.

" When he inquired of them what help he should have against the tempter, they replied, ' When you shall feel yourself afflicted by punishments, immediately call out and say, Jesus Christ, Son of the living God, have mercy on me, a sinner.' The monks referred to having retired, the demons forthwith appear, and at first flatter him with kind promises, saying that they should protect him and bring him back again in safety, if only he would obey them.

" But when he refused to obey them, immediately he hears the roaring of different wild beasts, which made him imagine that all the elements had clashed together, at which he exclaimed, with breathless terror, ' Jesus Christ, Son of the living God, have mercy on me,' &c., and forthwith this dreadful tumult ceased.

" Being conveyed thence to another place where also
there appeared a multitude of demons, saying to him—
' Do you imagine that you have escaped our hands? By
no means. But now you shall begin to be tortured and
afflicted the more.' And lo! a great and terrible fire
there appears, and the demons said to him—' Unless
you will submit to us, we shall cast you into this fire to
burn, which, when he refused, they took him and cast
him into the fire; but whilst he was there tortured, he
exclaimed, ' Jesus,' &c., and the fire at once became
extinguished.

" At length being led to another place, he beholds men
burning alive, and scourged by the demons with red-hot
iron plates, even to the very entrails, and crying out with
pain, ' spare us, spare us,' but the demons only scourged
them the more violently. Others he sees, whose limbs
serpents were devouring, and whose entrails were drawn
out by fiery hooks of iron; but as Nicholas would not
submit to their suggestions, he is cast into the same fire,
and is tormented by the same punishments, until he cried
out, ' Jesus, have mercy on me,' &c., and forthwith he is
liberated from his sufferings. Thence, being conveyed
to another place, he sees large pools of boiling metal, in
which some had one foot, others two : some were standing up to the knee in these pools, others up to the body,
and others to the breast, neck and eyes. Seeing all these
torments, he invoked the name of God, and passed
on to a wide pit, from which issued a horrible smoke and
a most intolerable stench. The demons told him—
' The place which you now behold is hell, in which our

master Beelzebub dwells, and into this abyss we shall
cast you if you do not yield to us; and after you shall
have been cast into it, you cannot find any means of
escape;' but as he spurned them, they seized him, and
cast him into the pit, where he was filled with such vehe-
ment torture, that he had almost forgotten to call upon the
name of God. After a moment, however, on recollecting
himself, he expressed the name of Jesus in his heart, as
he was unable to utter it with his lips, and immediately he
escaped uninjured, and the whole host of demons, being
completely vanquished, left him.

   " Having been led to another place, he sees a bridge,
over which it was necessary he should pass. This bridge
was very narrow and smooth, and slippery as ice. Underneath this bridge flowed a stream of sulphur and fire.
Then, recalling to mind the words that delivered him
from so many dangers, he approached with confidence,
and placing one foot on the bridge, he says, ' Jesus, have
mercy,' &c. Then there arose a loud cry, which so ter-
rified him that he could hardly keep his foothold till he
repeated the same prayer again, which he repeated at
each step, and thus crossed the bridge in safety.

   " Thence he reaches a most delightful meadow, where
the sweet odour of flowers charmed his senses. Here
two fair youths appear to him, and conduct him towards
a most beautiful city, resplendent with gold and gems.
From its gate issued the sweetest odour, which caused
him no longer to feel the sufferings and foul stench he
had just escaped. They told him that this city was
Paradise, into which Nicholas was most desirous to enter,

till the above-mentioned youths told him that he should first return to his kindred, pass through the places by which he had come—that the demons could not injure him, but would fly in terror at his sight—that in thirty days afterwards he should rest in peace, and then enter that city as a perpetual citizen.

"Then Nicholas, returning from the Purgatory, finds himself amongst his friends, and after telling them all that had happened to him, after the lapse of thirty days he calmly rested in the Lord."

This legend, as also that related of the Knight Owen, in the twelfth century, supplied the Spanish poet, Calderon, who lived in the seventeenth century, with the groundwork of one of the most charming of his sacred dramas. It is called *Purgatorio de San Patricio,* a metrical version of which was written by our poet-laureate, Denis Florence MacCarthy, and published in the year 1847. Longfellow's beautiful *Song of Hiawatha* closely corresponds with it in metre. As the concluding part of the *Purgatorio* of Calderon, where he represents the pilgrim after passing through the different stages of punishments, and arriving before the celestial paradise, is singularly sweet and interesting, I shall give it at some length :—

> "Ere I reached the gates they open'd,
> And the saints in long procession
> Came to meet me, men and women,
> Young and old, and youths and maidens.
> All approached serene and happy.
> Choirs of Seraphim and Angels,

Breathing heaven's delicious music,
Sweetly sung divinest anthems.
After these at length approached me
The resplendent, the most glorious,
The great Patrick, the Apostle.
Much that dazzling sight rejoiced me,
For by it I was enabled
To fulfil my early promise,
In my lifetime to behold him.
He and all the rest embraced me,
Pleased at my extreme good fortune.
Bidding me farewell, he told me
That no living man could enter
That most glorious, happy city;
But that I to earth returning,
Should await God's time and pleasure.
Back the proper way I wandered
Unobstructed by the demons,
And at length approached the entrance,
When you came to seek and see me.
Since I have escaped this danger,
Holy fathers, all I covet
Is to live and die among you."

CHAPTER XI.

DREADFUL TRAGEDY AT LOUGH DERG—RAYMOND COUNT
DE PERILLEAUX—THE DUTCH MONK—SUPPRESSION OF
THE CAVE ON SAINTS' ISLAND.

IN the year 1397, King Richard II. granted a safe conduct to Raymond, Count de Perilleaux, Knight of Rhodes and Chamberlain to the King of France, who came on pilgrimage to Lough Derg, accompanied by a retinue of twenty men and thirty horses. In connexion with this event a thrilling story is told in the *Dublin Penny Journal* of June 25th, 1836. It is there narrated how Count Raymond and another knight, named Ugolino, had been serving in the wars against the Moslems—that Ugolino had been the means of saving his life, and that at the close of the Crusade, Raymond persuaded Ugolino to accompany him to his home. Whilst there, notwithstanding the disparity of rank and family, a close intimacy sprung up between Ugolino and Raymond's sister, Madoline de Perilleaux. Raymond happening to find that they were pledged to marry, in a fit of passion plunged his dagger into his sister's breast, thus putting her to death for the honour of his house. Ugolino, when he found that she had been killed, vowed that he would never rest until that same poignard should pierce the breast of her murderer.

Count Raymond, tortured in conscience for his crime, proceeded on pilgrimage to Lough Derg, in order to appease the wrath of heaven. The story graphically proceeds :—" It was a beautiful evening in the autumn of 1397, and the flood of rich yellow light from the setting sun bathed the wooded shores of Lough Derg, tipping with gold the waves on its surface. At this time the naked hills, which now surround the lake, were covered with majestic woods of oak and beech,* and fringed with a thick copse of brushwood to the water's edge.

"The little island on which was situated St. Patrick's Purgatory, lay about a mile from the shore, resembling some dark spot in the midst of flowing silver.

" The ferryman was reposing on a grassy knoll at the verge of the lake, waiting to ferry over the pilgrims as they made their appearance. While he thus lay, with his beppeaᴏ (cap or hat) thrown over his eyes, to keep off the rays of the sun, a pilgrim, toiled and travel-stained, arrived at the bank, and stood beside the un-conscious ferryman. He was a fine tall young fellow, clad in the usual garb of a religious wanderer of the period. His face was thin and pale, but full of life and

---

* In a visit which the writer paid to Lough Derg, on the 4th September, 1877, he observed, on a portion of the mountain in the possession of a family named Gallagher, the stems and wide-spreading roots of two enormous fir trees, from above which the peaty surface had been cut. This is evidence that at a remote period, when our climate was much more temperate, large trees grew among these mountains, which are now so bare and barren.

animation. He was clad in the humble garments of a palmer, yet his mien and motion were those of one used to associate with the proud and noble. After a little the pilgrim pointed with his staff towards the island, as if indicating a wish to be ferried over, on which the ferryman directed his attention to the setting sun, as an intimation that the hour had passed, and then pointed to a cottage at the end of the wood, plainly intimating to the pilgrim that he should be content with a share of the shelter and hospitality of his humble roof till morning.

" The stranger bowed in thankfulness, laying the forefinger of his right hand impressively on his lips, and raising the other towards the blue vault of heaven. He then crossed both with an expressive gesture on his breast, and hung down his head in silence.

" ' Ay, ay !' uttered the boatman, in an undertone ; 'a vow to hold his peace—some terrible crime to be atoned for by the severity of the penance—and in one so young too ;' and with a glance upwards of astonishment and thankfulness to heaven, he led the way to his cabin. The evening sun had gone down behind the western hills, and the gloom of coming night was darkening the deep brown woods. The song of the robin and the thrush was hushed, and the pilgrim was seated beside the cheerful hearth of the ferryman, silent and motionless, and wrapt up in the shadowy stillness of profound meditation.

" On a sudden, however, the ferryman was startled on hearing the notes of a bugle-horn, which came pealing from the woods. He started to his feet, for such sounds were seldom heard on the peaceful shores of the Lake of

H

Penance, and on going out, he observed a train of horse-men issuing from the woods.

" The person who rode in front, and who appeared to be the chief, was mounted on a beautiful charger of the true Arabian breed. He was dressed in black. A mantle of velvet, lined with silk, depended from his shoulders, under which he wore a doublet of fine cloth, braided with twisted cords of silk, and fitting closely to the body. He also wore a broad-brimmed hat, from which drooped a solitary black feather, shadowing features proud, stern, and repulsive in their expression. The rest of the at-tendants were clad in much the same fashion, except a few, who were fully equipped and armed. They ap-peared as if after a long journey. They were evidently men from a foreign land, for they used much gesture, and spoke in a strange tongue. Tents were immediately pitched on the shores of the lake, and fires lighted, and a hurry and bustle continued among the strangers till a late hour, and a strict guard was placed on the pavilion of him who appeared to be their chief.

" Shortly after, the noble chieftain embarked for the island, and without an attendant, on reaching which, he hurried for the cell at which Raymond de Perilleaux was making his devotions. He advanced with a quick and rapid movement, till he came within a few feet of the holy shrine, at which he found him. He then called out in a loud exclamation :—

" ' We have met here alone, and face to face at last, Raymond, Count of Perilleaux. Can you pray to heaven ? You, with the blood of innocence crying to that heaven

for vengeance against you! Can you ask for pardon, or
hope for mercy, whose heart was closed against the plead-
ing of the virtuous and the innocent? Can you hope
for peace while my vow of revenge is unpaid, and the
dagger yet unstained with thy blood? Raymond of
Perilleaux, know you not that while I lived, my life was
devoted to your destruction? Now, say your last prayer,'
and he drew his blood-stained dagger.

" ' Mercy, mercy, Ugolino !' uttered Raymond, in a
trembling and distressed voice. It was all soon over ;
he raised up the dagger, and buried it to the very hilt in
the heart of the wretched count.

" The murdered victim never groaned—his lips were
seen to move in prayer; he staggered forward a few
paces, and fell heavily against the steps of the little
altar, where he expired."*

According to a pretty general opinion, or popular super-
stition, which prevailed amongst the peasantry of Ireland
down to recent times, wherever a murder or other tragic
event occurred, the spot where such murder was committed was supposed to be haunted for long after by the
ghost or spirit of the victim. Hence, such ghost-stories
are generally the most reliable traditional evidence re-
specting the commission of certain dark deeds, even at a
remote period, and often indicate the scene of such crimes
with the greatest precision.

---

*I have transcribed the abridged account of this tragedy as given
in that highly-interesting " Handbook of South-Western Donegal,"
the author of which is one of the most accomplished and esteemed
parish priests in " Old Tyrconnell."

The tragic death of Count Raymond also gave rise to
a ghost story at Lough Derg.   The local residents relate
that, down to modern times, a ghost, habited in the garb
of a pilgrim of the olden time, used to pace up and down
the island during the still hours of evening twilight.

This dreadful tragedy cast a gloom over Lough Derg;
and it would seem as if it were but the forerunner of a
train of evils which were to fall upon this sanctuary, and
which were to avenge the outraged majesty of God for
the desecration of His holy place.

Such repute did this western Purgatory acquire, that
about the period at which we have arrived, its bequests
and revenues had so increased as to afford ground, not
merely for grave responsibility in their administration, but
also for considerable jealousy as to their allocation.   Raymond Maguire, an Augustinian, was Prior of the Purgatory in the year 1455.   Donald M'Grath, who was probably coarb of the termonlands, and Thomas M'Creanyre,
Abbot of SS. Peter and Paul's at Armagh, probably on
account of his monastery having been the mother-house
of the establishment at Lough Derg, strove to prevent
Raymond Maguire, its Prior, from disposing of the proceeds from the Purgatory.   Maguire appealed to the Me-
tropolitan and to Rome, with the result that the community at Lough Derg were confirmed in their title to the religious offerings at the place, and the others were ordered,
under pain of excommunication, to give no further annoyance.

Under the year 1462, the Four Masters relate, that
" the Prior of Devenish, *i.e.*, Bartholomew, the son of

Hugh O'Flanagan, died at Lough Derg." This was the Prior who repaired or rebuilt the great Abbey Church of Devenish, as appears from the celebrated inscribed stone of Devenish, a full description of which will be found in that highly-interesting and valuable handbook, Wakeman's *Guide to Lough Erne.*

While the fame of St. Patrick's Purgatory had spread abroad, an incident occurred which for a time tended to mar its celebrity. A monk from Eymstede, in Holland, hearing of the fame of this western pilgrimage, and of the visions vouchsafed to the pious votaries at that retreat, as related in the poetic tales of the period, came to the determination of going thither, and of testing the accuracy of the sensational stories related of it. Having arrived at the island, the Prior, before admitting him to the cave, required that he should first obtain the Bishop's permission. The Bishop, in granting leave, required that he should pay the customary fee for admission. These fees were to be expended on keeping the churches and other buildings on the island in a suitable state of repair. The monk, now rendered doubly censorious and querulous, at length gained admittance to the cave, and expected, as a matter of course, that he should be favoured with the self-same visions with which others were said to have been privileged. His expectations, however, were not realized. The everyday painful exercises of penance were all the sights to be witnessed in this earthly Purgatory. Disappointed and chagrined, he went straight to Rome, and laid a most damaging report of the Purgatory before the Pontiff then reigning, Alex-

ander VI. He represented the exactions of the Prior,
Prince, and Bishop of the island—"*omnes enim petierunt
pecuniam.*" He mentioned his own experiences of it—
that he had not been favoured with those glimpses of
future punishment and bliss which were ascribed to it.
His words added force to prejudices already forming
against it over the Continent, and thus its temporary
suppression was determined upon, until such times as
the abuses complained of should be remedied.

In the "Annals of the Four Masters" there is found no
allusion to the closing of the cave on Saints' Island by
order of the Pope: mention is made of it, however, in
the "Annals of Ulster." The reason assigned by the
Bollandists and the "Annals of Ulster" for the suppression
of the cave are quite different. The Bollandists say
it was ordered to be closed because it had become " an
occasion of shameful avarice." It would appear as if
they grounded their opinion on the report of the monk
of Eymstede, which, however it may have precipitated
the action of Rome in the matter, we have yet to learn
whether it was the only cause to draw forth that decision.
The reason for its suppression, as set forth in the "Annals
of Ulster," I hold to be much more tenable, namely, "that
it was not the Purgatory which the Lord had shown to St.
Patrick." On this subject no better authority could be
adduced than the compiler of the Annals of Ulster, the
celebrated Cathal Maguire; for he was not only deeply
versed in his country's lore above all his contemporaries,
but was also, at the time of the edict in question, a high
dignitary and official of the diocese in which the Purga-

tory is situated; and, over and above all this, he was appointed by the Pope to assist in carrying out the Papal decree, and hence we may reasonably presume that he was fully acquainted with the causes which led to this decree.

In the words of the " Annals of Ulster :"—" A.D. 1497. The cave of Patrick's Purgatory in Lough Gerg, was destroyed about the festival of St. Patrick this year, by the Guardian of Donegal and by the representative of the Bishop in the deanery of Lough Erne " [*i.e.*, Cathal Maguire], " by authority of the Pope, the people in general having understood from the history of the knight, and other old books, that this was not the Purgatory which St. Patrick obtained from God, though the people in general were visiting it."

Now, as this Cathal or Charles Maguire was one of the most illustrious sons of the diocese of Clogher, and one of the most distinguished Irish ecclesiastics in any age, I will be pardoned for giving his obit as recorded by Roderick O'Cassidy in the " Annals of Ulster," which were brought by Maguire from A.D. 444 down to 1498, the year of his death, and continued by O'Cassidy to the year 1541. O'Cassidy writes :—" Anno Domini 1498. A great mournful news throughout all Ireland this year, viz., the following—Cathal Oge MacManus Maguire died this year. He was Canon Chorister at Armagh, and in the bishopric of Clogher, and Dean of Lough Erne, and Pastor of Inniskeen, in Lough Erne, and the representative of a Bishop " [*i.e.*, Vicar-General] " for fifteen years before his death. He was a precious stone,

a bright gem, a luminous star, a treasury of wisdom, and
a fruitful branch of the Canon; and a fountain of charity,
meekness, and mildness; a dove in purity of heart, and
a turtle in chastity; the person to whom the literati, and
the poor, and the destitute paupers of Ireland were most
thankful; one who was full of grace and wisdom in every
science to the time of his death, in law, physic, and
philosophy, and in all the Gaelic sciences; and one who
made, gathered, and collected this book from many other
books. He died of *Galar Breac* " (the small-pox) " on
the tenth of the calends of April, being Wednesday,
lxo. anno aetatis suae. And let every person, who shall
read and profit by this book, give a blessing on the soul
of MacManus (*i.e.*, Cathal Maguire)."

In the decree of Pope Alexander VI., we can observe
the vigilant care with which the Church guards her holy
places against even the least infringement of the established and authorized discipline. "Holy Church," says
one of our great writers, " neither admits nor encourages,
even by silence, anything contrary to truth, virtue, or
piety." Hence, in the case of Lough Derg, she did not
hesitate to interrupt that pilgrimage until the abuses complained of had been removed. But, as the interval during
which it was closed was only of short duration, we may
conclude that Rome soon after lent its sanction to the
place; and thus the pilgrimage, without further let or
hindrance from the ecclesiastical authorities, has ever
since maintained its salutary influence throughout the long
ordeal of persecution which swept over and laid desolate
most of the other religious institutions of our country.

CHAPTER XII.

HAT the Pilgrimage of St. Patrick's Purgatory remained closed but for a brief
period seems certain. It is stated that
George Cromer, Archbishop of Armagh,
made a strong appeal to Rome in favour
of its reopening; and that, acceding to
his solicitations, Pius III., who succeeded to the
Papacy in 1503, recalled the Bull of Pope Alexander, and issued another, granting indulgences to the
pilgrims and certain faculties to the community of Lough
Derg, which Bull has ever since continued in force·
Messingham (Florilegium, p. 125,) states that, on the
nature of its devotions being explained to the Holy See,
indulgences were attached to this pilgrimage before the
close of the sixteenth century.

So soon after the closing of the cave as 1504 we find
that the Prior in charge of it was the Rev. Turlough, or
Terence, Maguire, of whom the following notice is recorded in the *Annals of the Four Masters:*—"1504.

Turlough Maguire, who had been Canon Chorister at Clogher, Pastor of Derryvullen, and Prior of Lough Derg, fell down a stone staircase at the town of Athboy, about the Festival of St. Patrick, and died of the fall, and he was buried in the monastery of Cavan."*

Nor did the edict of Alexander VI. deter foreign pilgrims from visiting this sanctuary as of old, as we may fairly deduce from the following notable instance, taken from he Annals already referred to :—

"Anno 1516. A French knight came upon his pilgrimage to St. Patrick's Purgatory on Lough Gerg, and on his arrival and at his departure he visited O'Donnell, from whom he received great honours, gifts, and presents ; and they formed a great intimacy and friendship with each other, and the knight, upon hearing that the castle of Sligo was defended against O'Donnell, promised to send him a ship with great guns."

The question as to where the purgatorial cave was originally situated remains as yet surrounded with a good deal of uncertainty. By writers on the subject it is generally supposed to have been on Saints' Island ; but I am inclined to hold that, before the Augustinians became occupants of the place in the twelfth century, this cave was situated on the " Island of the Purgatory," now called Station Island. This opinion is supported by the authority of Giraldus Cambrensis, who, soon after Henry of Salffey's narrative had appeared, wrote an account of this country, in which he referred to Lough Derg. From

---

*In 1480 this was chosen as a burial place by his kinsman, Thomas Oge Maguire, an illustrious pilgrim.

this account it would appear that the cave was not in his time on Saints' Island, but on the smaller island, evidently the present Station Island. Other writers, also, inclined to the same opinion, though they may have rested their authority on Giraldus' statement. This conjecture is strengthened by the reason assigned in the *Annals of Ulster* for the closing of the cave—namely, that " it was not the cave shown by God to St. Patrick "— as well as by the fact that, after the decree of suppression, Station Island was thenceforward chosen as the place of pilgrimage. Hence we may fairly argue that the place of purgation or penance may have been originally, as at present, on Station Island ; here, too, St. Patrick may have prayed and done penance ; and here those visions regarding the future state of suffering and of bliss may have been witnessed. By accepting this opinion it would follow that the Canons Regular had established another *Caverna Purgatorii* on Saints' Island, for the twofold purpose of having it convenient to their monastery, and of saving themselves and the pilgrims from the difficulty and danger of the lake passage.

The Most Rev. Peter Lombard, Archbishop of Armagh, who wrote his *Commentarius de Regno Hiberniæ* in the year 1600—about a hundred years after the edict of suppression—says that in his time the guardianship of the Purgatory remained in the hands of the Augustinians, but the pilgrimage was conducted on Station Island. His words are :—" On the other island " (Saints' Island) " is a convent of St. Augustine, subject to the abbot and monastery of SS. Peter and Paul, situated in the see of

Armagh. Yet he, who on this lake is chief of the monks, is honoured with the title of Prior of the Purgatory. Two of these monks always reside in turn on the Island of the Purgatory, to receive and instruct, as spiritual fathers, those pilgrims who come there to expiate their sins."

And, speaking of the Island of the Purgatory—the present Station Island—the same Dr. Lombard writes: "In it are situated the ˉfollowing holy places, which are thus separate respectively from each other. In the first place, an elegant church, surrounded by a cemetery, in which church, along with certain other relics of St. Patrick, is preserved in the wall the stone on which the saint used to repose his head instead of a pillow. Secondly, a grotto a few paces to the north of the church, which is variously termed the Cave of the Purgatory, the Purgatory of St. Patrick, and even St. Patrick's Pit, which, though it is now almost on a level with the ground in its vicinity, was formerly of very great depth; but in the lapse of time and on different occasions, as tradition has it, both by the ordinance of successive bishops and with the approval of the Roman Pontiffs, it has thus become gradually raised to the surface of the earth about it. Its length, width, and height are such as to admit of twelve, or at most fourteen, persons arranged two and two in order, not standing erect, but profoundly inclined. Its walls and roof are of stone. At one side there is a small window, at which those bound to read the canonical hours are placed; and at its extreme end lies a stone, on which St. Patrick used to pray on bended knees, and which still retains the impression of his knees. This

stone covers the mouth of that dread abyss, which is said
to have been formed at the prayers of the saint. Thirdly,
beyond this cave, and facing the north, are seven cells or
stations, in memory of the more distinguished saints of
Ireland, which cells are called *lecti ponosi.* Fourthly, on
the opposite side of the church, towards the west, stand
some inns or cottages for the accommodation of the pilgrims." Dr. Lombard then proceeds to describe the
penitential devotions of the pilgrimage, which substantially correspond with accounts given by later writers,
hereafter to be noticed. His information regarding the
place he received from persons who made the pilgrimage
a few years previously. And he adds that the form of
penance there observed was practised by such numbers
that the English Deputy could neither prevent them nor
attempt to desecrate the place itself.

In this description, as given by Dr. Lombard, we have
a fair outline of Station Island as it was about three
hundred years ago. Allowing that the church of the
pilgrims stood where St. Mary's Church now stands ; that
the cave was situated convenient to the present campanile
(and this is confirmed by the remains of a narrow building, corresponding with the dimensions of the cave,
which may be seen at either side of the campanile, and
which tradition points to as part of the cave), which
would be certainly "a few paces to the north of the
church ;" that the penal beds held the same position they
now occupy, "beyond the cave, and facing the north ;"
that the inns or cells stood where the presbytery and line
of lodging-houses now stand, "on the opposite side of

the church, towards the west;" we are thus enabled to identify Dr. Lombard's outline and references. In his description what perplexes us most is his reference to a cemetery, seeing that the cemetery is situated on Saints' Island. Dr. Lombard, however, may have borrowed his phraseology from the situation of the church and cave in former times on Saints' Island, and to have drawn, in this instance, on the language of Henry of Saltrey, who describes the cave as being *in cœmeterio extra frontem ecclesiæ*. Besides, it is worthy of note that in opening the foundations of St. Mary's new church in 1870, human bones, some of which I have lately seen on the island, were discovered. These remains, which are in a remarkable state of preservation, would sustain the statement made by Dr. Lombard, that the church on Station Island had in his time a cemetery attached to it.

The topography of the Island of the Purgatory during the early part of the seventeenth century is also pretty accurately given in Sir James Ware's *Antiquities of Ireland* (London, 1654), where we find a description of St. Patrick's Purgatory, together with a map of the island on which the pilgrimage was then conducted. The island marked on his map must be Station Island; for he describes pretty accurately its extent as being scarce three-quarters of an Irish acre, whereas Saints' Island is fully ten times as large. This island is represented on his map as somewhat circular, whereas Station Island is in form an oblong strip of rock; but this may be accounted for by the circular appearance which it certainly presents from the shore of the lake. Ware thus describes the island, the church, the cave, and the circles or "beds :"—

"It is to be noted that the circles, commonly called 'beds,' enclosed with stone walls scarce three feet high, were the places where the pilgrims performed their penance. As to the cave itself, it was built of freestone, and covered with broad flags, and green turf laid over them. The door being shut, there is no light but what enters at a little window in the corner. It is in length, within the walls, sixteen feet and a-half, and in breadth two feet one inch. And as the cave itself is small, so likewise is the island, which is scarce three-quarters of an Irish acre. The church of the island was heretofore called *Regles*,* whether so from the relics there preserved, or because inhabited by Regular Canons, let others inquire."

On Sir James Ware's map are marked the Regles, or church—a cruciform building, the exact model and on the site of the old St. Mary's Church ; St. Patrick's Cross ; the *Caverna*, near it to the left ; *circulus vel lectus S. Brigidæ, lectus S. Catherinæ, S. Columbæ, S. Brendani, lectulus S. Abogi et Molasri et sti Patricii;* and there are also seven little lodging-houses represented round the margin of the island.

It would appear that the place of pilgrimage on Lough Derg, although territorially surrounded by the parish of Templecarn, formed in itself a distinct and separate jurisdiction from a very remote period. Originally, indeed, the community at Lough Derg may have

---

* A church erected by St. Columbkille at Derry was known as the Ouibh-Regler.

ministered to the spiritual wants of the district known as Termon-Magrath; but in the thirteenth or fourteenth century a parish church was erected at Templecarn, and a pastor appointed to the benefice, thus leaving the monks undivided charge of the monastery and of the pilgrimage. That this conjecture is well-founded would appear from the fact that in 1504 Turlough Maguire, who was Prior of Lough Derg, was then Pastor of *Derryvullen*, which clearly suggests that the priorate of Lough Derg and the pastorate of Termon-Magrath were two distinct offices and jurisdictions. Again, it is stated in the *Memoir of Most Rev. Peter Lombard*, by the Most Rev. Dr. Moran, that Hugh O'Neil, Earl of Tyrone, claimed and obtained from the Holy Father, in the year 1609, the restoration of the right of appointment to certain benefices, in the list of which Termon-Magrath is included. It is most unlikely, however, that the right of nominating the Prior of Lough Derg was included in that concession; whence it would seem to follow that Lough Derg was then, as now, a distinct jurisdiction. Nor can I find any record in ancient or modern times of any Pastor of Templecarn having been Prior of Lough Derg, of having exercised any parochial jurisdiction there, or of having exercised any spiritual jurisdiction there, except under the sanction and delegation of the bishop of the diocese. The Augustinian Canons conducted the pilgrimage till their expulsion in 1632. Next, Franciscan Friars had charge of it till towards the close of the last century, when the Bishop of Clogher (in which diocese Lough Derg lies) appointed one of the secular clergy of his diocese to officiate as prior. Since that time a prior and assistant confessors for the pilgrims are annually appointed by the bishop of the diocese. And it is but just to add that, under the paternal care of the bishop and clergy of Clogher, Lough Derg has flourished as a pilgrimage, maintained its hold on the affections of the faithful, braved triumphantly many obstacles and enemies, and, after centuries of persecution, still continues to be the proudest heritage of Ireland's faith and piety.

That Lough Derg was visited by great numbers of pilgrims during the sixteenth and seventeenth centuries, is put beyond doubt by the testimony of the Bollandists (March 17, p. 590), who say that in the sixteenth century it was visited by 1,500 pilgrims at the same time; and Archbishop Fleming, of Dublin, tells us that in 1625 many had to return without finding room to land on the island. I here insert the account of this pilgrimage, written by Dr. Fleming to the Internuncio at Brussels, on the 20th of August, 1625, from which we may infer what the course of penance at this pilgrimage then was :—

"The pious and innumerable pilgrimages of the faithful this year are a pledge of great fervour ; for, like bees to the beehive, there daily flock such numbers from every corner of the kingdom, for penitential purposes, to a certain island, which is called the Purgatory of St. Patrick, and which is situated in the centre of a lake, that many have been obliged to return without satisfying their pious desire, there being no room for landing on the island. This pilgrimage, though, through the bitter persecutions of heresy, it has been almost abandoned for many years,

I

was once so celebrated throughout the Christian world, that many from the most distant parts even of the Continent visited it in a spirit of devotion. The manner of performing the pilgrimage, as it is now observed from ancient tradition, is as follows :—Each person, from the day he arrives on the island till the tenth following day, never departs from it. All this time is, without intermission, devoted to fasting, watching, and prayer. If they wish to give rest to their body they must sleep on the bare ground, and for the most part under the broad canopy of heaven. They receive but one refection, and that consists of bread and water. It is incredible what severe austerities and bodily mortifications females, as well as men, and persons of every age and condition, endure whilst they perform this penitential course. During twenty-four hours they are shut up in certain caves, like unto prisons, where they pass the whole day and night, entirely absorbed in prayer, and receiving nothing to eat or to drink.

"I have thought it well to mention this fact, for I am sure your Excellency will be rejoiced to see that the natives of this island, by this so great and so unparalleled an impetus of devotion, seek to appease the anger of God ; and we may confidently hope that by their fervour He will be appeased, Who listens to the prayers of those who have recourse to Him in their afflictions."

The contemporary writer, Messingham (p. 95), describes the course of penance, as then performed on Lough Derg, more in detail :—"During the nine days of the pilgrimage," he says, "a rigorous fast was observed on oaten bread and water of the lake. The pilgrim was first conducted barefoot to the Church of St. Patrick, around which he moved on his knees, seven times inside and seven times outside, repeating all the while stated prayers of the Church. He was then conducted to seven places, or stations, known as *lecti poenosi*, which were formerly small churches, or sanctuaries, dedicated to various saints ; and at each of these he repeated the visit as above. The next station was around a cross in the cemetery, and subsequently at another cross that was fixed in a mound of stones. Thence he proceeded, over a rough and rocky path, to a spot on the border of the lake, to which tradition pointed as the place on which St. Patrick had knelt in prayer. Here also certain prayers were appointed to be recited. All this pilgrimage and prayer was repeated three times each day—morning, noon, and evening—during the first seven days ; on the eighth day it was repeated six times ; confession and communion followed on the morning of the ninth day ; and then the pilgrims entered the cave, where twenty-four hours were devoted to fasting and meditation. Any that chose not to enter the cave passed these twenty-four hours in solitude at one of the former stations."

Carve states that, besides their fasting, watching, and other bodily austerities, the pilgrims offered prayers to God for the common welfare of the Church, and for the preservation of true peace and concord amongst all Christians.

But the darkest day in the history of Lough Derg is drawing near, when the Calvinists, under Government orders, desecrated and demolished this sanctuary, on which Primate Lombard bestowed the distinguished title of being "the most celebrated and holy place in Ireland;" when the apostate English determined to destroy that shrine of religion, where their forefathers in the Ages of Faith had done penance ; where King Aldfred of Northumbria had prayed to St. Patrick before his return to England from the schools of Mayo and Lisgoole ; and where Harold, afterwards King of England (not to speak of many other princes and nobles of that country, who had done likewise), made pilgrimage about the year 1050 to the "miraculous cave of St. Patrick." Of the doom which awaited Lough Derg at the hands of the Calvinists, let the following chapter bear evidence.

CHAPTER XIII.

DESTRUCTION OF THE RELIGIOUS ESTABLISHMENT ON
LOUGH DERG—EXPULSION OF THE AUGUSTINIAN MONKS
—GROUND-PLAN AND DESCRIPTION OF THE RUINS ON
SAINTS' ISLAND—DR. KIRWAN, BISHOP OF KILLALA,
PILGRIM AND CONFESSOR AT LOUGH DERG—TESTIMONY
OF THE NUNCIO RINUCCINI IN ITS FAVOUR—THE BELL
OF ST. DABHEOC.

ROM an inquisition, taken at Donegal in the first year of the reign of James I., and copied by O'Donovan into his *Donegal Letters*, it would appear that the Augustinians were driven from Lough Derg, and their monastery and church pulled down, even before the year 1632. The document in question runs thus:—" In the parts of Ulster, near the territory called O'Donnell's Countrie, are the walls and monuments of a certain monastery, or priory, late house of the Canonical Friars, called the Priory of Loughdarge, *alias* commonly called 'St. Patrick's Purgatory;' which priory now is very much on the decay, and has these many years past been totally abandoned and dissolved. The aforesaid priory lies and is situate in a certain small island in the middle of a lake, called Lochdarg, about fifteen miles from the village of Donnagall aforesaid. The prior of the monastery afore-

said, at the time of the dissolution and abandoning aforesaid, was seized as of fee, in right of the priory aforesaid,
of the site, circuit, ambit, and precinct of the said late
house, with the appurtenances, in which are an old
church very ruinous, and walls of stone lately levelled,
with small piece of land circumjacent, containing one
and a-half acres of land ; and of the whole island aforesaid,
containing about ten acres; and of certain lands and
hereditaments to the said house and island adjacent,
called Termon-Magrath and Termon-McMonghan, containing four quarters of land of the great measure."
That the absence of the Augustinians from this establishment was but temporary, and in consequence of the persecution then setting in against this stronghold of Catholic
piety, we may infer from the testimony of Dr. Lombard,
as also from the report of Sir William Stewart, who found
there an abbot and forty friars in 1632. From the foregoing document we can easily understand how the English
garrison at that time in Ireland, well aware of King
James' hostility to the Catholic religion, lost no time in
visiting with destruction this sacred retreat, in testifying
their zeal for the work of the Reformation, and in com-
forting the Royal conscience by sending forward this
very favourable report.

We have already seen how, with the troubadours, poets,
and romancists of the middle ages, Lough Derg had
become the theme of poetic tales ; and how legends and
stories regarding it formed part of the sensational literature of the period. In these tales poetic imagination
conducted those who visited the island of Lough Derg,

at first to the regions of Purgatory, and afterwards to the abodes of the blessed or of the damned. At the outbreak of the so-called Reformation, Protestant writers seized on these legends and tales, as if they were matters of fact, and made use of them in order to cast ridicule on the pious practices of the Catholic Church. By degrees they began to level their attacks on this time-honoured sanctuary. In the beginning of the reign of James I. they demolished its churches and oratories. But, despite their efforts, the faithful still continued to flock to it in great numbers, which so enraged the enemies of our faith that the Lords-Justices, on the 13th of September, 1632, made a last effort to destroy this pilgrimage. The author of the *Monasticon Hibernicon* states that it was in the year 1630 the Government of Ireland decided on having it finally suppressed, and he adds—" It was accordingly dug up, to the no small distress and loss of the Roman Catholic clergy."

For some centuries before the period at which we have arrived, the Magraths of Termon-Dabheoc were hereditary guardians of the lands assigned to the sanctuary of Lough Derg. Their family residence was a strong keep or castle, known as the Castle of Termon-Magrath, the ruins of which yet remain a short distance below Pettigo, to the left of the line of railway from Enniskillen to Bundoran. · The only portion of the parish of Templecarn and county of Donegal bordering on Lough Erne is close to this old keep of the Magraths. The soil here is very rich ; and what with wooded shores, lake, islands, and lofty mountains, the visitor will here behold the most charming scenery in the north-west of Ireland. The tradition is still kept that this castle was built by the famous Miler Magrath, the eldest son of Donogh, otherwise Gillamagna Magrath of Termon-Magrath, of which that family had been crenachs. If built by him, it was probably before his apostasy, which took place at Drogheda, on the 31st of May, 1567. During his four or five months' possession of the temporalities of Clogher, as its first Protestant bishop, it is likely he ventured not to revisit the family residence, but took up his abode at Ballymacann (Ferdross?), near Clogher. That this patrimony of Lough Derg escaped the grasp of the so-called Reformers down to the reign of Charles I. is certain.

During this reign the representatives of government in Ireland, after publicly announcing that, in the opinion of the "Papists," there was a passage from this island to the other world, and an entrance to the realms of purgatory, issued orders to have the whole island dug up, and that especially no portion of the cave should remain undestroyed. With this object the Lord-Justice Boyle ordered Sir James Balfour and Sir William Stewart to seize unto his Majesty's use the Island of Purgatory.

On the 12th of September, 1632, the very day before the Government orders were carried out at Lough Derg, a messenger came from Donegal to forewarn the monks of their impending fate. He communicated to them, as a local tradition has it, what he overheard amongst the military at Donegal, and besought them to escape in time, and thus save themselves from their enemies. The monks, however, determined to remain at their post, and calmly to await the consequences. In the meantime, familiar as they now were to such hostile visitations, they made ready for the worst, having first secreted in a safe hiding-place in the ground the more cumbrous articles of value—reserving only for removal such articles as they might bring with them without attracting the notice of the greedy soldiery. At length, after a night of sorrow and suspense, the morning of their expulsion dawned ; and as the day advanced a company of cavalry from Donegal was observed making their way over the mountains, and advancing quickly towards the lake. In the most summary way possible they ordered the venerable abbot and his community, which consisted of forty monks—"all fine, able men," as my informant traditionally learned—to take their departure. A detachment of soldiers was directed to escort the monks as far as Portcreevy Bay, to make sure of their departure, and to prevent them from being eye-witnesses of that ruthless destruction, which had already befallen their consecrated abode. The afflicted monks, having taken their last look, and, as it proved, their last farewell of Lough Derg, proceeded, we may suppose, towards Devenish, Lisgoole, and Clones, where flourished houses of their order, and where stood guest-houses or hospices, which for centuries past were chiefly occupied by pilgrims to Lough Derg.

As to the manner in which the Government orders were carried out, Sir William Stewart informed the Privy Council that, on proceeding to Lough Derg, "he found there an abbot and forty monks, and that there was a daily resort of four hundred and fifty pilgrims, who paid eightpence each for admission to the island. He further states that, in order to prevent the seduced people from going any longer to this stronghold of Purgatory, and wholly to take away the abuse hereafter, he had directed the whole to be defaced and utterly demolished. Therefore, the walls, works, foundations, vaults, &c., he ordered to be rooted up; also the place called St. Patrick's Bed, and the stone on which he knelt. These and all other superstitious relics he ordered to be thrown into the lake, and he made James Magrath, the owner of the island, to enter into recognizances that he should not in future permit the entrance of Jesuits, friars, nuns, or any other superstitious order of Popery to enter therein."*

To aggravate the atrocity of this act of vandalism, it is related that Knox, whom James I. dubbed Bishop of Raphoe, witnessed from the shore of the lake and encouraged by his presence the work of destruction—a proceeding which completely casts in shade the sacrilege of the Protestant Archbishop, who unroofed the buildings on the Rock of Cashel.

But 'mid weal and woe the Irish heart had entwined round the holy island of Lough Derg. Though the Augustinian Canons were not destined to return to Saints' Island, a place of residence for the officiating priests was erected on Station Island; the ruined church and crosses and oratories were again put in some sort of repair by loving hands; and the pilgrimage rose again, phœnix-like, from its ashes.

---

* Taken from Rev. Cæsar Otway's *Sketches in Donegal.*

SAINT'S ISLAND, LOUGH DERG.

W.F. WAKEMAN.

Before tracing the onward progress of the pilgrimage on Station Island, I think it will not be unacceptable to give a sketch and outline of the ruins on Saints' Island, which have suffered little from the hand of man for the last two hundred and forty-six years. And, even making allowance for the "wear and tear of time," they remain in much the same state in which they were left by the Puritan soldiers of 1632.

The accompanying engraving of Saints' Island, which was sketched by W. F. Wakeman, Esq., of Enniskillen, on the 4th of September, 1877, will convey a pretty accurate idea of how complete was the work of the destroyer, as neither buildings nor ruined walls are to be observed on it. In order to obtain a favourable view for this sketch, we rowed out some distance from Saints' Island, in the direction of Station Island. Here in the background appeared, on the one side, Meenanellison, which signifies the *mountain meadow of the little fort* (this fort being still observable there) ; and on the other side, Croagh Breac—*i.e., the speckled stack mountain*—which derives its name from the numerous gray crags that here and there jut out from among the heather, giving it in reality this speckled appearance.

On the southern shore of Saints' Island the stone piers, on which rested a bridge of beams, are still to be seen. Between these piers there is a channel about twenty yards wide, and from twenty to thirty feet in depth ; and through this channel flows a strong current from the upper lake. Some twenty yards down this channel a boatman on the lake, not long since, observed two fir-beams, with iron cranks attached ; the inference being that they formed part of the old bridge, and were washed down the bed of the channel by the force of the current.

A short distance to the west of this bridge, on the mainland, and at the very shore, may be seen the foundation-stones of an old building, the enclosure being completely filled with the fallen walls. Tradition points this out as the ferry-house of Teague O'Doherty, whose name yet lives in the folklore of the locality. It is also said that Teague had charge of the ferry from Portcreevy to Station Island—remains of his boat-quay at Portcreevy being yet in very good order, where a goodly sprinkling of oak, ash, and sycamore trees lends a sylvan charm to this once-frequented harbour. For four or five generations O'Dohertys lived on the slopes of Augh-Keen mountain ; but they are long since extinct in that locality.

On the very summit of Saints' Island portion of the old ᴜᴩ, which we have already referred to in Chapter V. of this work, may be seen. Immediately adjoining it, on the eastern side, is the cemetery, which measures thirty-five yards in length, by twenty-seven yards in width. It was surrounded by a strong wall, now very much in ruin. In the centre of the cemetery may be seen the dilapidated remains of a very small structure. It measures externally, as far as I could make out, eighteen or nineteen feet in length, by about twelve feet in width. This was very probably the *Caverna Purgatorii*, though on the Ordnance Map it is marked towards the eastern extremity of the island ; for it corresponds with the dimensions of this ancient cave, and agrees also with the description given of it by Saltrey and others, who state that it was situated *in cœmeterio extra frontem ecclesiæ.* About twelve feet west of this structure I observed a circular heap of stones, which may have been the former *situs* of St. Patrick's Cross, hereafter to be noticed. Immediately adjoining this structure, on its northern side, a long flagstone covers what tradition points out as the grave of a friar. East of the cemetery, but quite convenient to it, there are two circular heaps of stones, which may have been saints' "beds" in former times. The space here is enclosed by an earthen fence, and south of this enclosure, what would seem to have been a garden extended, which terminates in a long terrace beside the shore of the lake. Woodbine and willows now fringe this terrace, forcibly reminding us of that striking line in Goldsmith's "Auburn":—

"Near yonder copse, where once a garden smiled."

On the eastern declivity of the island, between the cemetery and the shore, are the ruins of what I suppose to have been the church of the pilgrimage. The walls now remaining are only about two or three feet high, and its measurements are thirty-six feet long by twenty-six in width. Immediately adjoining this church is an open space enclosed by a wall, also in a very ruined condition, which measures sixty-six yards round the enclosure. This wall of enclosure is six-sided, and I strongly suspect that the seven penitential beds of the pilgrimage were within this. Behind this sexangular enclosure, a round hollow may be observed in the ground. It is almost filled up with earth, and is seldom to be seen without water. Tradition states that this was the Pilgrims' Well, and that the pilgrims used here perform their ablutions before departing from Saints' Island.

At the eastern extremity of the island large quantities of building material have been thrown down the slope of the bank. Here it is said the monastery stood; but everything is in such a ruined state as to baffle identification or trace of either walls or foundations. The trees and bushes, which have here taken such deep root, render it an easy matter for rabbits (here so numerous) to burrow amongst the *debris*, thus adding to the ruin already existing. The natives of Lough Derg relate how treasure-seekers tore up the ruins at the eastern shore of the lake, as it was supposed the monks buried here their valuables. This story may have been occasioned by the search which a certain Frenchman (of whom more hereafter) is said to have made here for the ancient Purgatorium. An underground passage is said to have connected the monastery with the church; and from the church to the cemetery a narrow cloister, which is still quite distinct, extended. Amongst the *debris* referred to, some freestone coigns, door-blocks, and flags, well dressed and chiselled, are to be found; and it is said that many of the ornamental cut stones on Saints' Island were long since carried off by peasants throughout the surrounding mountains, and converted to mean and profane purposes—a species of vandalism that cannot be too highly reprobated.

A little farther down the bank, facing Station Island and bordering on the margin of the lake, stood a small building, the object of which I cannot conjecture. It measured fifteen feet in width, by twenty-two in length.

It should be added that Saints' Island was enclosed all round by an earthen fence ; and in addition to this, at the eastern extremity, there was an outer wall of enclosure (the outline of which is still discernible), built a few yards from the shore, out in the shallow water, and reaching round the eastern extremity of the island. This wall, which is of horseshoe form, has a convenient landing-place at either extremity, and from its extremities a strong earthen fence ran across the ridge of the island, thus securely enclosing the church and monastery. Amongst the natives of Lough Derg the opinion prevails that the purgatorial cave was situated at or near the eastern extremity of Saints' Island, where the large quantity of rubbish lies scattered about. The Ordnance Survey party, strange to say, confounded it with the church of the pilgrimage, which they have marked as the Purgatory. But the opinion I have already advanced as to its site—namely, that it corresponds with the little ruined structure in the middle of the cemetery—is, I think, the most tenable.

From the outline we have given of Saints' Island, we hope that pilgrims and tourists will be enabled to form a pretty fair estimate of the extent and celebrity of the pilgrimage, whilst here conducted ; as also to recognise the singular interposition of Divine Providence, which has enabled it to survive so many vicissitudes and so much persecution.

During the reign of James II. respite was afforded to the pilgrimage. A church with a thatched roof—its dimensions 40 by 11 feet—was erected, having an aisle

on the south side 16 feet square. This church was
ruinous in 1727, when Richardson wrote of it; but, he
says, the aisle was then lately repaired.　The presbytery
and cabins for the pilgrims were equally humble, and
quite in keeping with the church.　Hence it does not
surprise us to hear that the winter storms each year had
such ruinous effect on them, and that at the opening of
each station such labour was needed to put them in
suitable repair.

In the Life of Dr. Kirwan, Bishop of Killala, by John
Lynch, Archdeacon of Tuam, and first printed in 1669,*
we have a faithful description of the austerities then
endured at this penitential retreat, as well as of the
motives which induced the faithful to flock thither in
such numbers.　Dr. Lynch writes :—" That he " (Dr.
Kirwan) " might not be wanting in any species of piety,
he reverenced in his soul the custom of undertaking
pilgrimages.　Nor was he satisfied with visiting such
places in Connaught as were consecrated by the sojourn
of the saints, and, above all, the rugged mountain called
Cruagh-Padrick, which he was wont to frequent. . . .
But often, too, did he go into Ulster, to the far-famed
Purgatory of St. Patrick, in which the pilgrims were wont
to abstain from meat for nine days, using no food save a
little bread and water from the lake.　During one of the
nine days they are shut up in the dismal darkness of a
cavern, and, therein fasting, partake of nothing save a
little water to moisten their throats when parched with

---

* This work, called *Icon Antistitis*, was republished with a translation in 1848 by Rev. C. P. Meehan.

thirst. At noontide and evening they go on bended knees over paths beaten by the feet of saints, and strewn with sharp stones. In other quarters they walk barefooted over rugged ways, in the olden time frequented by holy men to satisfy for their transgressions. Sometimes walking and sometimes on their knees, they advance to a considerable distance into the water. Thus do they spend the day, pouring out their prayers to God, and listening to holy discourses; nor in this sacred place is there to be seen or heard anything scurrilous or ludicrous. When night comes on they lie down, not to enjoy repose, but to snatch a few moments' sleep; their beds are of straw, nor do they use any pillow but their garments. Thrice each day did Francis, with the other pilgrims, punctually perform these duties, and, in addition, he diligently applied himself to hearing confessions and preaching sermons."

One of the most favourable testimonies regarding the renown and sanctity of this pilgrimage is that furnished by the Papal Nuncio, Rinuccini, in the report of his nunciature, made to the Holy See on his return to Rome in 1649. After stating how much he desired to rescue from the hands of the heretics the far-famed Purgatory of St. Patrick, he adds :—" The devotions of this deep cave are of great antiquity, though their first origin is uncertain. It is agreed that the saint chose that spot for his holy retreats ; and the visions with which he was there favoured by God, were well known and approved of by succeeding generations. At present the fury of the Calvinists has levelled everything with the ground, and

K

filled up the cave ; and thus they destroyed every vestige
of the spot, so do they seek to cancel every trace of its
memory.   It seemed to me that my mission from Rome
should embrace this, too, as one of its special objects ;
and I would have been, in part, content, could I have
planted the cross on that island.   But I was not blessed
with the fulfilment of this design."*

The Rev. John Richardson, Rector of Belturbet, in
the year 1727 wrote an account of Lough Derg, entitled
the *Folly of Pilgrimages* (a most bigoted and hostile production), in which he relates that a certain Frenchman,
named Ludovicus Pyrhus, of Bretagne, came to Lough
Derg about the year 1693, for the purpose of discovering
the ancient purgatorial cave.   Mr. Richardson's words
are :—" In order to do this he employed labourers to dig
and search for it throughout both these islands, the
neighbouring priests giving their assistance.   He continued two summers at this work, and after he had spent
all the money he brought with him, fell a trafficking, and
applied the profit to the same use.   At last, as he was
searching among the rubbish of a dwelling-house in the
largest island " (Saints' Island), " he found a window with
iron stanchers.   Mr. Art MacCullen, Popish priest of
the parish ; Mr. Mark MacGrath, and Mr. James Max-
well, a Protestant, who gave me this account, being
present.   There happened to be a dark cavity under the
window, and, after digging a little deeper, they found it
to be a cellar window; whereupon Ludovicus Pyrhus
ceased from searching any more, and returned to his

---

*Nunziatura, p. 414.

native country. Among the rubbish they found a little bell, which is now in the College of Dublin; and an image, which is said to be the image of Caoranach, and is kept on the lesser island for the satisfaction of the pilgrims."

Whether this Ludovicus Pyrhus had been in search of the ancient purgatorial cave, or, rather, of the valuables secreted here by the Augustinian monks, I cannot say; but it would seem that this incident it was which gave rise to the popular tradition still existing here, namely, that a good many years ago treasure-seekers had torn up the ruins at the eastern extremity of Saints' Island, but failed to discover the much-coveted treasure-trove.

The bell said to have been found in the ruins on Saints' Island by Ludovicus Pyrhus was probably the Bell of St. Dabheoc. I have heard that many years ago a square bronze bell, purporting to be St. Dabheoc's Bell, was preserved on one of the altars at Lough Derg; but there is now no trace or record of its whereabouts. If this be the bell found by Ludovicus Pyrhus—and it is very likely—then, if it be true that in Mr. Richardson's time it was preserved in the "College of Dublin" (*i.e.*, Trinity College), I think it may yet be discovered.

The other object of antiquity, namely, the image of Caoranach, found in the cellar on Saints' Island, is still preserved on Station Island. This is an image or representation, cut in stone, of that fabulous monster, called by some Caol, by others Caoranach, which, before its destruction by St. Patrick, is said to have been such a cause of terror to this whole neighbourhood. This mythological figure somewhat resembles a wolf with a serpent's tail entwined around it. On the stone on which it is cut Father Anthony O'Doherty, of the Order of St. Francis, inscribed the date and purpose of a house which he founded here in the year 1763, for the accommodation of the Franciscan Friars then ministering to the pilgrimage. The stone, with this figure and inscription, is preserved in the southern gable of St. Patrick's Church on Station Island; and we shall hereafter have occasion to refer to its inscription.

As we have already described the expulsion of the Augustinian Canons, and the destruction of their monastery on the " Holy Island," we shall consider in the next chapter the progress of this pilgrimage under their pious successors, the Franciscans.

CHAPTER XIV.

THE FRANCISCAN FRIARS AT LOUGH DERG—CONFISCATION
AND ALIENATION OF THE POSSESSIONS OF THIS PIL-
GRIMAGE—WRITINGS AGAINST IT—THE ENACTMENT OF
QUEEN ANNE—ST. PATRICK'S CROSS—BISHOP HUGH
M'MAHON VISITS THE SANCTUARY—SERMON OF BENE-
DICT XIII. ON ST. PATRICK'S PURGATORY—DR. DE BURGO
AND TURLOUGH O'CAROLAN PILGRIMS TO THIS SANC-
TUARY.

HEN the community of the Franciscan
Monastery at Donegal were forced to
abandon their cloisters in 1601, the
greater part of them found a home and a
refuge in Louvain, Brussels, and Antwerp.
Yet some of them preferred remaining in
their native country, hoping that the dawn of
better days might see them restored to their
plundered home by the banks of the Esk. Of these we
may suppose some afforded the consolations of religion
to their persecuted fellow-countrymen ; whilst others, to
supply the void created by the expulsion of the Augustinians, volunteered their services in the difficult and
dangerous office of ministering to the pilgrims, who still
came flocking to the ruined sanctuary of Lough Derg
About the time in question, many of the Augustinian
houses in the north of Ireland had passed into the hands

of the Franciscans; many of the missionary clergy were also Franciscans, and even some of the bishops. In a *Relation* of the northern dioceses by Primate Oliver Plunket, dated March 6th, 1675, we find the following reference to Clogher and Raphoe, which fully carries out what we have said regarding the Franciscans :—" The diocese of Clogher is about fifty miles long and sixteen wide; it has thirty-five parish priests, two convents of the Franciscans, and one of the Dominicans. The bishop is Dr. Patrick Duffy, formerly a Franciscan friar." Of Raphoe it is said that it has one Franciscan convent. From these convents, we may rightly conclude, some of the friars were deputed each season to minister to the spiritual wants of the pilgrims, as down to the time of Father Anthony O'Doherty (1763) the friars do not appear to have had a permanent residence on the island. Towards the latter part of the seventeenth century, amongst the Franciscans labouring at Lough Derg, should be mentioned Friar Conway, who was a maternal relative of Mr. Edward Nicholson, of Manchester (of whom more hereafter). It is probable the Rev. Art MacCullen and the Rev. Mark M'Grath, who assisted Ludovicus Pyrhus in his explorations, were also Franciscans. When Bishop Hugh M'Mahon visited the island in 1714, he found the Franciscans in charge; and later on, in the eighteenth century, we find Father M'Grath and Father O'Doherty, Franciscans, in charge of it.

We have already seen that the church-lands of Lough Derg were vested in the Magraths of Termon-Dabheoc; and that, at the expulsion of the Augustinians in 1632,

James M'Grath was confirmed in this office, under certain conditions and stipulations. It appears that this James M'Grath was friendly towards the pilgrimage, if we are to give credit to Richardson, who states that in 1727 there stood, on the south-eastern part of Station Island, "St. Patrick's Altar," with an old cross within a circle on it, inscribed—*Jacobus M'Grath fieri fecit*, 1632.* It is stated in the Auchinleek MSS. that this James M'Grath afterwards disposed of his right in these termon-lands to Dr. Spottiswood, Protestant Bishop of Clogher (who died in 1644). The extract from the Auchinleck MSS. runs thus :—" Nowe had the Bishopp " (Dr. Spottiswood) " gott eight or nyne Townelandes lying contigue to his new howse in Clogher, which he destinat to be a perpetuall Demeasnes for his succeeding Bishopps, and gott an Act of Estate past thereon. He recovered also other lands his predecessor, Bishopp Montgomerie, was never in possession of; as, namelie, the Isle of Devenish, from the Lord Hastings ; the greatest part of the Island of Inishmore, from Sir Ralph Goore, Baronet ; the lands of Termongrathe, from James Magrath," &c.† These termon-lands thus became part of the see-lands of the Protestant bishops of Clogher ; and probably at the union of this bishopric with Armagh by Act of Parliament (1834), they were purchased by Mr. Leslie, of Glasslough, County Monaghan (who was the lineal descendant of Dr. John Leslie, fifth Protestant Bishop of Clogher), their

---

*Of this inscription I could find no trace at the island.
†See Rev. W. H. Bradshaw's *Enniskillen Long Ago*.

present owner being Sir John Leslie, Bart., of Castle-Leslie, Glasslough.

The pilgrimage of Lough Derg very much exercised the zeal of the Protestant bishops of Clogher. Dr. James Spottiswood wrote a treatise on it, intituled *St. Patrick's Purgatory*. His successor, Dr. Henry Jones, also took it to task in his *Patrick's Purgatory* (London, 1647). Richardson, in his *Folly of Pilgrimages* (Dublin, 1727), acknowledges in his preface to that work the helps he received from the " present and late bishops of Clogher. The draught of the whole island, and of all the superstitious things *(sic)* in it, was sent to me by Bishop Ashe, being made by an ingenious and worthy clergyman, the Rev. Joseph Story, pursuant to his lordship's direction." We also find that the Rev. Philip Skelton, Rector of Fintona (in his works, 6 vols., Dublin, 1770), dedicated his *Account of Lough Derg* to the then Protestant Bishop of Clogher (probably Dr. Robert Clayton, of Arian notoriety). We may here include the *Description of St. Patrick's Purgatory*, by the Rev. Mr. Hewson, Protestant Archdeacon of Armagh (Dublin, 1727).

Of all these and kindred notices written of, or rather against, this pilgrimage in the seventeenth and eighteenth centuries, we are bound in justice to observe that they are all animated by a similar spirit of hostility to this institution of Catholic piety ; and they clearly show how the Protestant clergy, not content with seeing its churches and cloisters levelled with the dust, still continued to pour out the vials of their wrath upon its ruins, and sought to hold up to the ridicule of the iconoclasts of 1632 and

their sympathizers the devotion and piety of the persecuted faithful, who, albeit their many privations and sufferings, found consolation for their souls in the austere
penances of this holy retreat.

From the destruction of the sanctuary of Lough Derg,
in 1632, down to the second year of the reign of Queen
Anne (1704), the pilgrimage continued each year increasing in the number of its pilgrims, and in its reputation for sanctity. In this year, however, an Act was
passed prohibiting pilgrimages in general, but especially
that of St. Patrick's Purgatory, in the following words :—
" And whereas the superstitions of Popery are greatly
increased and upheld by the pretended sanctity of places,
especially of a place called St. Patrick's Purgatory, in the
County of Donegal, and of wells, to which pilgrimages
are made by vast numbers at certain seasons . . . . .
Be it further enacted, that all such meetings and
assemblies shall be deemed and adjudged riots and
unlawful assemblies, and punishable as such, in all or any
persons meeting at such places as aforesaid. And all
sheriffs, justices of the peace, and other magistrates, are
hereby required to be diligent in putting the laws in force
against all offenders in the above particulars in due
execution." And further on in the same enactment it is
decreed that a fine of ten shillings be inflicted on any
offender, and, in default of payment, that he be publicly
whipped. Also that persons who at such assemblies
build booths or cabins for the sale of victuals or any
other commodity, shall forfeit and pay the sum of twenty
shillings, to be forthwith levied by distress. The docu-

ment thus concludes :—" And all and every the said
magistrates are hereby required to demolish all crosses,
pictures, and inscriptions that are anywhere publicly set
up, and are the occasions of Popish superstitions."

Regarding the numbers making the pilgrimage in the
commencement of the eighteenth century, the Rev. Mr.
Hewson, who wrote his account of St. Patrick's Purgatory, on the 1st of August, 1701, says :—" There were
near 5,000 there last year, as the Prior told me, who
registers their names ; but not 2,000 had been this year,
when I was there, and commonly more men than
women." And he afterwards adds—" There were about
300 of these devotees (sixty of which were in the caves)
when I was there." The better to put a stop to the pilgrimage, the mountain district leading to Lough Derg
was " planted " by Protestant settlers. In this district,
extending from Pettigo to Lough Derg, the posterity of
these settlers remain to this day ; and, though in former
times they and their co-religionists in the neighbouring
counties gave the utmost annoyance to the poor pilgrims,
they are now kindly disposed towards the pilgrimage.

One of the oldest relics of the ancient sanctuary of
Lough Derg is the Cross of St. Patrick. This undoubtedly
stood on Saints' Island when the religious establishment
was there ; and, judging from its style and art, dates as
far back as the twelfth century at least, though Mr.
Wakeman seems to think it may be as old as the ninth
century. The sketch of this cross (which we here present to our readers), drawn on the spot by Mr. Wakeman
on the 4th of September, 1877, and engraved by Mrs.

Millard, includes also the fragment of St. Dabheoc's
Cross, described at page 43 of this work. St. Patrick's
Cross exhibits more art, and consequently must be of a
later date than the fragment referred to ; yet it cannot be
questioned that it also is of great antiquity. The shaft of

St. Patrick's Cross, Station Island.

St. Patrick's Cross on Station Island is octagonal at the
base and capital; between the base and capital it is
circular, with a raised band of spiral tracery running
round it. Its dimensions are—Height of shaft between
capital and pedestal, 3ft. 7in. ; height of capital, 4½in. ;

diameter of capital, 8in.   The capital is formed by three
raised parallel bands and two hollow ones running round
it octagonally.   A small portion of the capital has been
broken off; as also the shaft a little above the pedestal,
which, however, is kept together by means of a strong
iron band or clasp.   Evidently it was thus broken when
the iconoclasts invaded Saints' Island, and it still presents
the most forcible proof of how complete was the work of
the destroyer.   This cross is set into a mound of stones,
or *circulus*, near the southern gable of St. Patrick's, or
" Prison " Chapel.   Clearly this shaft was surmounted by
a stone cross, which rested in the hollow space which
still remains at the top of it.   This was broken, but in its
place there is a plain iron cross, made fast by lead.
Round this cross the usual *ex votis* shreds and offerings may
be seen suspended.   The popular legend relative to this
cross is that it was transferred miraculously from Saints'
Island, where it formerly stood ; and that the event confirmed the selection of Station Island as the place of
pilgrimage.   The statement* that this stone cross is the
identical Clogh-Oir, is so reckless and unsupported by
the least evidence as not to deserve any notice ; for even
the merest tyro in Irish history knows full well that the
Clogh-Oir stood at the royal and ecclesiastical city of
Clogher ; and it is still pointed out leaning against the
side of the Protestant church at that place.

What incalculable good Lough Derg has contributed
to religion and morality since its origin, and with what

---

*This statement has been hazarded in the *Irish Monthly*, January
number, 1878.

oil of comfort it soothed the bleeding wounds of our persecuted country during the long and dismal penal days, will never be fully realized till the great Accounting Day. The learned Balmez, in his *European Civilization*, speaking of the advantage to society of the retreats of the solitaries, and of pilgrimage thereto, justly says :—" It is impossible not to understand how much these communications must have contributed to correct and elevate ideas relating to religion and morality, and to amend and purify morals." Notwithstanding the enactments so cruelly enforced against this venerable retreat, it still remained firmly as ever rooted in the hearts and affections of the Irish race; it has outlived the penal days, and still continues to flourish with increasing life and renewed vigour.

To give the names of all the distinguished persons who made pilgrimage to Lough Derg within the last two hundred years would, indeed, fill many a page. Though no regular registry of them has been preserved, yet the names of some of the most distinguished amongst them we have been able to glean from different sources. From the *Irish Ecclesiastical Record*, vol. i., No. 10 (a source on which I have drawn for many facts and documents in this work), we learn that Dr. Hugh M'Mahon, Bishop of Clogher,* presented to the Sacred Congregation a *Relatio*

---

*He was appointed to Clogher in 1707, and translated to Armagh in 1715. In Dr. Renehan's *Collections* he is erroneously marked as appointed to Clogher in 1708, and translated to Armagh in 1709. In the same work he is said to have been the brother of his successors in the primacy, Bernard and Ross, whereas he was but their uncle.

Status of the diocese of Clogher ; and, amongst other matters, refers in detail to the pilgrimage of Lough Derg, of which he had personal experience.   He visited the Island of Lough Derg in the disguise of a merchant from Dublin ; for, owing to the temper of the times, it was not yet safe for a bishop of the Catholic Church to appear in public.   I here give a translation of the Latin copy as given in the *Record*, from which it will be seen that certain changes had been introduced into the ritual of the pilgrimage since the time when Peter Lombard wrote of it.   This most important document runs thus :—

" In the northern part of this diocese of Clogher, that most celebrated place, commonly called St. Patrick's Purgatory, is situated, in a small island, completely surrounded by a lake, towards which, from the beginning of June till the end of August, there crowd each year, from all parts, even the most remote, of this kingdom, thousands of men and women of every age and condition, who there spend nine days, living on one meal each day of oaten bread and water.   They lie upon the cold ground, walk barefoot, and their feet are frequently cut and bleeding.   Thrice each day do they visit the different stations over a rough path strewn with sharp pebbles, a considerable part of which is covered with water knee-deep.   At length, on the ninth day, having first made a general confession, having expiated all the faults of their life, and being nourished with the Bread of Life, they enter before twilight a subterraneous pit, which is called the purgatory, and here they remain four-and-twenty continuous hours, all the time awake and engaged in prayer, without any refreshment either of food or drink. When the same hour arrives on the following day they go forth, and dip their heads thrice in the cold water. And thus is completed that pilgrimage, to which idle inventors of fables have added so many exaggerations about spectres and visions, which never had any existence save in the distorted imagination of such story-tellers. For the three months during which this pilgrimage lasts, Masses are celebrated from dawn till midday; confessions are heard; twice or three times each day a sermon is addressed to the people, who, with copious tears, sobs, lamentations, and other marks of penance, frequently interrupt the preacher. And with such sweetness of interior grace does our most merciful Lord enrich this arduous and very austere pilgrimage, that they who before appeared obdurate and plunged in the mire of vice, come to feel the strongest stings of compunction. Nor are they satisfied with approaching this island once or twice; for I have found in this diocese persons who made the pilgrimage as often as fourteen times. The plenary indulgence accorded by the Holy Father, Pope Clement X., to those visiting this pilgrimage (which will soon expire, and requires a renewal), has added no small increase to the fervour of the pious pilgrims. It is regarded by all as little short of a prodigy how this pilgrimage, though prohibited by name, in the foremost place, and under the most severe penalties by Act of Parliament, suffered little or no interruption from the bitter Scotch Calvinists living in the neighbourhood and elsewhere. When I myself visited the place, under the guise of a Dublin merchant (for under the disguise of a trader or tradesman the prelates and non-registered priests of this country generally find it necessary to conceal themselves), the minister of that district received me very kindly. Though everywhere else throughout the kingdom the ecclesiastical functions have ceased, on account of the prevailing persecution; in this island, as if it were placed in another orb, the exercise of religion is free and public, which is ascribed to a special favour of Divine Providence, and to the merits of St. Patrick. When I was there, an English Protestant, induced by the fame of the place and out of curiosity, came there; and, being moved to compunction at the example of the penitents, forthwith abjured heresy. The Franciscan Fathers, beyond all the other ecclesiastics who came there, labour the most strenuously. At this pilgrimage I remarked one custom (not to call it an abuse), namely, that they who are about to enter the cave have Mass celebrated for them, which is always a *missa de requiem*, just as if they were dead to the world, and ready for sepulture; which, when I was anxious to abrogate, at least on Sundays and the principal festivals, on which should be said the Mass conformable to the office, they claimed the authority of immemorial possession and of custom to the contrary, first originated, as tradition says, by St. Patrick himself; which, being constantly asserted by learned and scrupulous men, has perplexed me, and therefore I beg to be instructed by your Eminences as to what I am to do thereon."

Soon after Dr. M'Mahon sent his *Relatio* to Rome, supplicating a renewal of the indulgences accorded to this

pilgrimage by the Sovereign Pontiff, the Cardinal Archbishop of Benevento, subsequently raised to the Papal
chair under the name of Benedict XIII., addressed a
homily to his flock on the subject of St. Patrick's Purgatory. The Most Rev. Dr. Donnelly, Bishop of
Clogher, when attending the sessions of the Vatican
Council in 1870, saw in the library of St. Clement's
Dominican Convent, Rome, a copy of the sermon which
Benedict XIII., while yet Cardinal, preached in praise of
this pilgrimage. The sermon is classed Number 13
amongst several other sermons treating of the various
purgatories, or places of purgation, throughout the world.
Since the time of Benedict XIII. the devotions of this
pilgrimage have been specially cherished and encouraged
by the Holy See.

In the year 1748 that learned prelate of the Irish
Church, Dr. Thomas De Burgo, author of the *Hibernia
Dominicana*, visited Lough Derg, and in that work gives
us his impressions of it :—" So great," he says, "are the
penitential deeds performed there, that they exceed, in
my opinion, those of any other pilgrimage in the world."
And he adds :—"I do not relate mere matters of hear-
say, but what I have witnessed with my own eyes ; for I
had the great happiness to visit, in the year 1748, that
island, which was consecrated by the habitation and
miracles of the most holy Patrick, and which still affords
an illustrious example of the austere penances of the
primitive ages of the Church " *(Hib. Dom., p. 4, et seq.).*
He says that each pilgrim repeats each day the Lord's
Prayer and Angelical Salutation nearly three hundred

L

times, the Apostles' Creed about one hundred times, together with the entire Rosary of the Blessed Virgin three times. He further states that the pilgrims, by going through each station, travelled over the distance of two miles.

Some time before this, the exact year is not recorded, another distinguished Irishman came here on pilgrimage. This was no less a personage than Turlough O'Carolan, " the last of the bards "—

" Who erst our halls with melody did fill."*

The remains of O'Carolan (as stated in Hardiman's *Minstrelsy)* await the final resurrection in Kilronan, the church of the Duigenan family, in MacDermott Roe's vault. In his youth the bard became acquainted with one Bridget Cruise, but he afterwards got married to Mary Maguire, of the Maguires of Tempo—once a noble and powerful family, but now quite degenerate. The well-authenticated tradition still lives at Lough Derg how O'Carolan, when old and blind, occupied the pilgrims' boat on his return from the island. At the landing-place a number of the pilgrims were eager to offer their services to the helpless one to land. O'Carolan had no sooner touched a hand, which was stretchèd out to guide him, than he paused for a moment, and exclaimed with emotion, " This is the hand of Bridget Cruise." And Bridget Cruise, indeed, it was, to whose praise his harp had first resounded, who stood before him, and the clasp

---

*For an account of his last resting-place see *The Legend of Kil-ronan,* by " Lageniensis " (Dollard, Dublin, 1877).

of whose hand he had recognised, though they had not met for years ! On this subject the late Samuel Lover, of facetious and harmonious memory, has written a charming song, sung to the sweetest of airs, from which I here cull the following stanza :—

> " When the minstrel sat alone,
>   There that lady fair had gone ;
>   Within his hand she placed her own.
>   The bard dropped on his knee,
>   From his lips soft blessings came,
>   In trembling tones he named—her name,
>   Though he could not see."

CHAPTER XV.

INSCRIPTIONS OF THE EIGHTEENTH CENTURY AT LOUGH
DERG—VOTIVE GIFTS TO THE SANCTUARY—ST. PATRICK'S
CHURCH—BOAT ACCIDENTS ON LOUGH DERG—MELAN-
CHOLY BOAT ACCIDENT OF 1795—PRIOR MURRAY—BRIEF
REVIEW OF THE PILGRIMAGE DURING THE EIGHTEENTH
CENTURY.

E have already referred to the inscribed
stones, which are set, for preservation, in
the southern gable of St. Patrick's Church,
on Station Island. Two of these inscriptions are given at pages 51 and 53 of this
work ; and from them we may reasonably
conjecture that a Franciscan Friar, named Father
Magrath, was Prior here in 1753. These two
inscribed stones were originally placed within two of the
penal "beds," or circles, on this island. Side by side
with these stones, in the same wall, is placed that most
ancient and most valuable inscribed stone, which is fully
described in chapter viii. of this work.

In addition to these is the stone with the figure of
Caoranach, *in alto relievo* (already referred to). Before
this mythical representation a cross is inscribed, and
underneath it the following inscription, in the quaint style
of the period :—

" Ys house
was built Fr. Anth : Do
herty for ye use of
ye Conv : of Donegal
his age 68 ye 8 Sep :
A:D: 1763."

From this it would appear that Father Anthony
O'Doherty was Prior of the island at the date mentioned—
namely, the 8th of September, 1763. In that valuable
handbook named *South-Western Donegal* (already referred to), we find that this same Father O'Doherty came
by one of the silver chalices, which is said to have formerly belonged to the Donegal Convent, in which convent, as appears from Father Purcell's account, given by
the Rev. C. P. Meehan, " there were sixteen silver
chalices, all of which, two excepted, were washed with
gold." On this chalice the following inscription appears :—

" *Fr. Ants. O'Doherty, T.S.D. procuravit*
Hunc Calicem pro usu fratrum minorum
Sanctae nostrae fraternitatis
Conventus Dongaliensis."

That this chalice was used in the celebration of the
Divine Mysteries at Lough Derg we can hardly doubt.
In 1850 it was brought to America by the Rev. John
Donnelly, whose native place adjoined the venerable and
historic churchyard of Aghalurcher, County Fermanagh.
At his death the chalice came into the possession of the
Rev. Edward M'Gowan, of Penn Yann, U.S.A., who
presented it to the Rev. Mr. Stephens, P.P., Killybegs, in
whose keeping it now remains.

Another of the Lough Derg chalices is that long preserved at Corduff chapel, parish of Carrickmacross. This
was a votive offering made to the sanctuary of Lough
Derg by a lady named Clara Nugent, *alias* Cusack, of
Carlanstown, in the County Meath. She was closely
related to Dr. Thomas Dease, Bishop of Meath, whose
mother was Lady Eleanor Nugent, of Carlanstown, a
noble branch of the family of Delvin. How this chalice
came to Corduff I cannot say, if it be not that the altar
plate of Lough Derg was removed for better security, at
the close of each station, to the episcopal residence,
during the time when three of the bishops of Clogher
found a secure abode within the loyal and devoted
" Dominion" of Farney. This small silver chalice is of
great beauty of workmanship, chaste and simple in
design, and of very graceful proportions. Its measurements are—Height, 6¾in.; diameter of cup, 2¾in.;
pedestal, 3¾in. in diameter. On the upper part of the
pedestal of this chalice a crucifix is inscribed; underneath
it the following legend :—

" *Clara Nugent, als Cusack de Carlanstown, pro Loghdarig
me fieri fecit, 1721.*"

On the outside of the cup is inscribed a harp indistinct,
also a harp with crown. On the principle that *res clamat
dominum,* we venture to express a hope that these chalices
may again be restored to the sanctuary of Lough Derg.

During the summer of 1878 another inscribed stone
was discovered in the floor of one of the cabins on the
island, and for its preservation it was set in the wall of

St. Patrick's Church, along with the stones already noticed. Its inscription reads :—

> *" Permissu Superiorum,*
> *Pro publico bono conditoris,*
> *Antonius O'Flaherty.*
> *A.D. 1763."*

We have no means of knowing who this Anthony O'Flaherty was. He was probably of the lordly family of the O'Flaherties of H-Iar Connaught, who, in the day of their power, were friends and benefactors of many a church and cloister. It is clear he rendered invaluable aid and assistance in the erection of buildings at the pilgrimage, in conjunction with the Prior, Father O'Doherty, for which service permission was obtained to erect a stone on the island to perpetuate the memory of his pious liberality. What the buildings at this time erected were I cannot positively say. It seems most likely that St. Mary's Church, which was replaced about forty-nine years after by a new structure, was one of the buildings then erected. To this conclusion I am led mainly by a " Map or Plan of the Island, and of St. Patrick's Purgatory," which I find in the *Antiquities of Ireland*, by Edward Ledwich (Dublin, 1790). Here we have " the church, or monastery," marked near the present site of St. Mary's—but a little to the west of it. The date-stone of this old church was found in the walls of St. Mary's Church, which were taken down in 1870 to make room for the fine Gothic edifice which now crowns its site. Though not at all ancient, yet I think this

inscription certainly belongs to the last century. Unfor-
tunately, the date of the year in which it was erected is
broken off this stone, thus leaving us somewhat in doubt.
It is set, the same as the others, in the gable wall of St.
Patrick's Church.   The inscription reads :—

> " THIS : CHAP :
> WAS : DEDI
> CATED. TO
> Ye : B:V:M:
> OF ANGELS
> & CONSECᴅ
> JULY : Ye 20."

Our conjecture is that this latter inscription was the
titulus or date-stone of the church erected at this time by
Friar O'Doherty ; and that the stone first noticed in this
chapter was erected in an aisle attached to this church,
which was used as a dwelling-house by the officiating
clergymen ; whilst the stone commemorating Anthony
O'Flaherty may have been erected in an oratory or chapel
raised by him over " St. Patrick's Altar,"* which, according to Hewson and others, stood at the farther end of
Station Island.

The purgatorial cave down to the year 1781 or 1782
(the year of the Catholic Relief Act) was, according to
Richardson, " 10 feet distant from the church ; it was 22
feet long, 2 feet 1 inch wide, and 3 feet high.   It hath a
bending within six feet of the far end, where there is a
very small window, or spike-hole, to let in some light and

---

*Called by Richardson the " Altar of Confession."

air to the pilgrims that are shut up in it. There is little or none of it under ground, and it seems never to have been sunk deeper than the rock. It is built of stone and clay, huddled together, covered with broad stones, and all overlaid with earth." This cave was closed up about the year 1781 by the Prior, who considered it insufficient for the number of persons who sought admission to it. A new church, 72 feet long by 24 wide, called St. Patrick's Church, or " Prison" Chapel, so-called from the fact that it was intended to supersede and serve the purpose of the ancient purgatorial cave, was built about this time. This church was re-roofed and slated in 1796 by the then Prior, the Rev. Mr. Murray. With the exception of the following additions and repairs, it is still substantially the same church as that erected in 1781. In 1835 an aisle was added to it by the Rev. Patrick Moyna. In 1860 it was remodelled internally ; its galleries, which were approached by stone steps from the outside of the gables, were removed, besides other very necessary improvements effected by the Rev. John M'Kenna. Further extensive repairs have been made to it during the summer of 1878 by the Rev. James M'Kenna, P.P., Aughavea.

Taking into account what angry storms sometimes sweep over the lake, lashing its waves into great fury, it is a merciful dispensation of Providence that more accidents have not occurred here ; and this more especially when we consider not only the proximity of the Atlantic, which is but five or six miles west of it, as likewise the high elevation of the lake itself above the level of the sea, but also the frail nature of the barks, which in days gone by

used to ply over its waters. Whilst the religious establishment stood on Saints' Island, there is no tradition of
any boat accident having occurred, though the barks then
in use were currachs, or canoe-shaped boats, formed out
of a hollowed tree.

Many years ago, it is handed down, two priests went
out for a sail on the lake, in a boat of the latter description; and when but a short distance south of Station
Island, where there is a round rock almost hidden under
water (since called "The Priests' Rock"), the boat capsized, and its occupants were drowned. This, they say,
was the first boat accident on Lough Derg.

A second boat was lost here, between Saints' Island
and the River Fluchlynn, about forty years ago. The
boatman was Doherty, from Augh-Keen, who, in company with two or three others, were returning home
from Kelly's Islands in the month of March, when the
boat, which was small and unsafe, capsized a little from
land, and all met with a watery grave; not even Doherty,
who was a good swimmer, being able to escape. This sad
accident inspired the muse of a local bard, who com-
memorated the event in a mournful lay, still sung in the
locality.

But the most lamentable catastrophe of all happened
here in 1795—a catastrophe which for many years cast a
gloom over the place, and the recital of which, even yet,
fails not to evoke from the pious pilgrims many a tear
and prayer for those who met with such an untimely end.
Sunday, the 12th of July, 1795, is a day long to be
remembered in connection with Lough Derg. On that

day, which set in fresh and breezy, but by no means
very stormy, there was the usual bustle and hurry about
the " cabin," or ferryhouse, from an early hour of the
morning, amongst pilgrims and the neighbouring inhabitants, who were anxious to hear Mass on the island. A
few boats had already taken full cargoes to and fro, when
the dread hour of eleven o'clock arrived.   Johnston, the
ferryman, had already allotted place for ninety-three passengers, all told, most of whom were pilgrims.   It appears that some of the passengers took exception to the
boat, as being old and unseaworthy ; but their fears were
made light of.   A very fortunate escape is related of a
young man, a pilgrim, who had actually taken his seat in
the boat, when he was summoned back by his father, who
had dreamt the previous night of some terrible fate about
to befall his son, followed him to the lake, and thus
saved him from certain death.

At about the hour of eleven o'clock MacTeague, the
principal boatman (who is said to have been somewhat
under the influence of drink at the time), pushed off from
shore, and all went well till they came alongside Prior's
Island.   At this time it was observed that the boat had
sprung a leak, and was fast taking in water.   The boatmen, however, took no heed of this, thinking they could
reach Station Island without any difficulty.   As they had
reached about midway between Prior's Island and Station
Island, the water was now fast gaining on the boat,
which alarmed the passengers, and rendered them quite
restive.   In this confusion and dismay the boat capsized,
and all went down in about ten feet of water.   It is said

that at this time they were so convenient to Station
Island that nine or ten good strokes of the oars would
have easily taken them to land.   Station Island itself at
the time was crowded with spectators, who were so
thunderstruck by the accident that they had not the presence of mind to push off to the rescue, though a boat or
two were within reach at the island.   If this had been
done, there is no doubt whatever but that very many of
the victims might have been saved.   It is consoling to
record that one of the priests then on the island waded
out some distance into the water, gave conditional absolution to those drowning, and repeated aloud certain
prayers for the occasion.   All the priests then on the
island offered up Mass for the souls of the deceased ; and
the Prior (Father Murray) is said to have declared, in a
funeral oration on the occasion, that had the accident
happened them when leaving the island, there would be
room for more consolation indeed.

A few moments after the capsizing of the boat, a large
mass of human beings, having grasped each other with
the tenacity of death at the bottom of the lake, came to
the surface, where they remained struggling for a little,
when they sank to rise no more.   Out of the ninety-three
passengers but three escaped—one of them a man named
Mulharty ; the others were a man and his mother-in-law
from the County Monaghan.   The boatmen were also
lost, as well as some of the people of the neighbourhood,
who were going to hear Mass on the island.

At the time the accident occurred it is said that Johnston, the ferryman, was giving tickets at the ferry-house

to a batch of fresh arrivals; he is reported to have made
light of the matter, and to have said that it would by no
means prevent the station from proceeding as usual.

All the bodies of those drowned were recovered from
their watery grave. Many of them were conveyed home
by their sorrowing friends to the family burial-places.
About twenty or more of them were buried coffinless on
the topmost part of Prior's Island, earth having been
carried up and heaped over their grave; and here a dense
cluster of firs may be observed waving their sombre
heads over their lonely grave. Others of them, again,
were buried in Templecarn churchyard. The sight of
the dead bodies, as they were conveyed on horseback
over the rugged mountain, was most heartrending; and
those who witnessed the sad ordeal (and there are some
of them still alive in the vicinity of Lough Derg) could
never after refer to the subject without shuddering at the
recollection of it.

In connection with this sad accident a remarkable
instance—if instances were wanting—is handed down of
the affection and veneration of the Irish for their departed
relatives. It is said how a young girl, the only child of
her widowed mother, happened to be in the ill-fated boat,
was drowned, and her body was buried in Templecarn
graveyard. The following summer her aged parent came
nearly one hundred miles to perform the "station" for
her, and brought with her a monument, which she had
erected over her daughter's grave in Templecarn. This
monument, or gravestone, is, I understand, still pointed
out to the visitor.

Though these were the only boat accidents known to
have taken place at Lough Derg, yet there were times,
some of which are fresh in my memory, when the pilgrims' boat ran considerable risk from the waves, and
when the skill and energy of such experienced boatmen
as Pat M'Kane, of Seeavoc, were taxed to the utmost in
making headway against the triple waves, which are, I
believe, peculiar to this lake.   There were days also, but
very few, when, owing to the storm, the work of ferrying
the pilgrims had to be suspended, and when the pilgrims
approaching the lake had to find shelter as best they
mig' t in the "cabin" by the shore.   I cannot help
thinking that, with no very great expenditure, a small
steamboat might be provided for the accommodation of
this pilgrimage, which would thus render the work of
transit not only more expeditious, but also quite secure
in every state of the weather.   If this were an English or
a Continental lake, instead of an Irish one, can we doubt
but that its waters would be traversed by yacht and
steamer, and that hotels and villas would look down from
the surrounding heights on its delightful expanse of
water ?

    We have seen that the old cave or caves (there being
at times two or more of them) had been superseded about
1782—the year of the passing of the Catholic Relief Act—
and a commodious church, called St. Patrick's Church,
erected to supply its purpose, as well as to serve for
general worship.   Who built this church I cannot say, if
it be not Father Murray, P.P., of Errigle-Truagh, who
about this time became Prior, in the room of the Fran-

ciscans, who, owing to the reduction of their numbers, could no longer minister to the pilgrimage. Whether this church was erected by Father Murray or not, it is certain that he slated and repaired it in 1796—the year after the boat accident. From his venerated successor in the parish of Truagh, I have it that Father Murray had not then the luxury of a church in his own parish, having to rest satisfied with those substitutes, then pretty common, called " Mass-gardens." He is described as of a mild and quiet disposition, and with the close of the century his term of office as Prior of the pilgrimage drew also to a close.

Towards the latter part of the eighteenth century the course of penance at Lough Derg was considerably modified. The incarceration in the cave or prison, which formerly lasted during twenty-four hours, was now reduced to twelve hours. The period of remaining on the island, which formerly extended to nine, or at least six days, was now reduced to three days. Since this time three days constitute the term of a station, though cases are not unfrequent where pilgrims remain on the island for six, or even nine days.

Hewson says that in his time (1701) "there were many priests in the island, and every day they have a sermon preached in Irish, about one o'clock." Richardson (1727) says there were twenty-four priests engaged there every station season. But this is probably an exaggeration. Skelton says that in 1770 there were about 4,000 pilgrims annually frequenting the island ; and he states that the pilgrims had then sufficient shelter and accommodation

on the island.   Immediately before the boat accident of
1795, the arrivals each season must have reached the high
figure of between ten and fifteen thousand.   The boat
accident, however, together with other reasons, which we
shall notice hereafter, caused the influx of pilgrims at the
close of the century to become considerably reduced.
Yet, through all its vicissitudes, the Holy Island continued still to be regarded with love and devotion by the
faithful children of St. Patrick, who before this sanctuary
renewed themselves in piety and the love of God.

CHAPTER XVI.

THE PILGRIM-TAX—THE FERRY-MEN—THE MOST REV. DR.
MURPHY'S REGULATIONS FOR THE PILGRIMAGE—RE-
SCRIPT FROM ROME—ST. MARY'S CHURCH—THE PRESBY-
TERY—HOSTILE NOTICES OF THE PILGRIMAGE—PRIORS
SINCE THE YEAR 1800—INFLUX OF PILGRIMS—THE
FAREWELL ODE TO LOUGH DERG.

ONE of the most remarkable remnants of
the feudal laws, or of the penal laws (it
matters little which), that I know of, is the
tax or tariff which each pilgrim has to pay
towards the "lord of the soil" for the
privilege of obtaining access to the Island
of Lough Derg! Not content with obtaining
possession of the lands given as a perpetual
endowment to this sanctuary, and of which it held undis-
puted control for over a thousand years, the Protestant
bishops of Clogher, after doing their utmost to disparage
and to utterly exterminate this pilgrimage, formed the
idea of turning it to profitable account, by exacting from
each pilgrim a fine for liberty to approach the shrine of
his devotion. And thus they who in theory condemned
this institution, did not hesitate in practice to appropriate
to themselves this iniquitous tax.

The more easily and the more securely to collect this

M

tax, the ferry was rented at a fixed annual sum to a
ferryman, who, after paying the stipulated amount to his
master, had to depend on the balance of the proceeds
for his own behalf.   The rent of the ferry generally rose
or fell according to the number of pilgrims visiting the
island; so that from the rent imposed each year we may
form a proximate idea of the number of arrivals at this
sanctuary.   Towards the latter part of the last century a
Protestant family of the name of Johnston rented the
ferry at £250 each year.   About the beginning of this
century one of these Johnstons, who was the ferryman,
gave great dissatisfaction, as we shall afterwards see.
After him a man named Travers managed the ferry for
about ten years.   Next came Robert Johnston, who
rented the ferry down till 1844.   At this time Catholic
ferrymen came into office, the first of whom was Daniel
Campbell, who conducted the ferry in 1845.   After him
his son John, who rebuilt the ferry-house and also erected
a building on the island, which was never completed.   It
reverted next to his brother, Peter Campbell; then to his
brother William, who held it down to the year 1862-3,
when Thomas Flood, of Pettigo, got charge of it.   He
held it till 1876, when his brother Patrick (the present
ferryman) secured his right in the ferry.   The rent of the
ferry was reduced for the Campbells to £150; and since
then it has been still further reduced to £50, which is
the present rent of the ferry, yearly payable to the present
owner of Termon-Dabheoc—Sir John Leslie, Bart., M.P.

In order to make up this tax, a fine of 6½d. was formerly imposed on each pilgrim for the "right of way" to

the island. Latterly, however, in consequence of the diminished number of pilgrims, it was deemed necessary to raise this tariff to 8d.

In May, 1798, Dr. James Murphy was appointed Coadjutor Bishop of Clogher, and on the death of Bishop Hugh O'Reilly (November 3rd, 1801) succeeded to the mitre of Clogher *per coadjutoriam*. One of his first cares was to look after the administration of the pilgrimage of Lough Derg ; and with this object in view he addressed a list of regulations to the Prior, Father Bellew, and his principal assistant, the Rev. Peter M'Ginn. The document in question is headed—" A few of the many regulations necessary for the orderly administration of the Station of Lough Derg," and bears date—" Tydavnet, May 26th, 1802." This document sets out with a regulation which for many years was strictly adhered to, but which is now obsolete ; and it is as follows :—

" I hereby prohibit, under pain of suspension *ipso facto*, any confessor already approved, or who may be approved of this season for Lough Derg, not excepting even the Prior himself, to receive the confession, give the absolution, or admit to the indulgence of the Station of Lough Derg, any pilgrim or penitent who has not complied with his Easter duty this year in his own parish, or who cannot produce a certificate, signed by his own parish priest or ordinary confessor, permitting him to be admitted to the benefit of said indulgence, though he has not complied with said Easter duty.

" And further, I hereby order, under the same pain of suspension, said certificate to be submitted to the Prior for his approbation of its authenticity before the bearer of it is admitted to confession," &c.

After giving other regulations regarding investing the pilgrims with cords, scapulars, and other religious badges ; also with regard to the selling or blessing of such religious badges, &c. ; and likewise concerning the allocation and discharging of intentions for Masses received on the island, next comes the following regulation :—

" Fourthly—This regulation regards the teaching of the Catechism on the Island of Lough Derg."

And the communication thus concludes :—

" As these, however, or any other regulations that may be adopted, must prove useless if the Messrs. Johnston and their boatmen persevere in their monopolies and in their severities towards the clergy and stationers, you will take care to speak to and settle matters with them if you can ; otherwise suspend the station instanter."

What the particular severities and monopolies here complained of against the Johnstons were, I have not learned; but I heard that they established "patterns" at the shore of the lake, where music, dancing, and drinking were introduced, thus tending to bring the place into disrepute, and giving great annoyance and scandal. Father Bellew, however, grappled at once with this difficulty, immediately put a stop to these "patterns," and by his energy and prudence upheld the discipline and order of the pilgrimage. Unlike the first of these Johnstons, who was so harsh and severe towards the pilgrims, and who is said to have admitted to the island all visitors ndiscriminately, against the orders and remonstrances of the Prior, the last of the Johnstons, namely, Robert Johnston, was, on the other hand, both courteous towards the pilgrims and amenable to the wishes of the Prior.

With regard to the admission of visitors, the rule at present observed is—that visitors be furnished with written permission from the Prior before the ferryman is at liberty to land them on the island. The reasonableness of this rule will be apparent to all when they consider how limited is the area of the island, how much both priests and pilgrims are occupied with their respective duties, and how much frequent visits of this sort would interrupt and distract the devotional exercises of the pilgrims.

One of Dr. Murphy's regulations, as we have seen, enjoined the teaching of the Catechism on the island. For this purpose two catechists were retained here for many years, one of whom taught the Irish Catechism, the other the English Catechism. Besides instructing the rude and illiterate in their Christian doctrine, these catechists lent valuable aid to the clergy in helping to prepare and dispose the pilgrims for the sacraments. In addition to these were the Prior's Clerk and also the Director of Devotions, whose special duty it was to maintain order during the night of the " prison," or " vigil."

Early in the year 1805 Bishop Murphy applied to the Holy See for a renewal of the usual faculties and indulgences attached to this pilgrimage, to be available for the space of fifteen years. Cardinal Jugnani, Secretary of the Sacred Office, sent a rescript to Dr. Murphy, bearing date the 16th of March, 1805. From this rescript we give the extracts bearing on our subject :—

"*Tam vero supplicem libellum Amplitudinis tuæ nomine R. P. Magister Lucas Concanen,** Ordinis Praedicatorum, ad nos detulit, quo postulabas, ut indulgentiæ ad quindennium pro stationibus peregrinationis, quæ Purgatorium Sti. Patritii appellatur impertitæ, ad illud quindennium renoventur. At quoniam in Archivis hujusce S. Congregationis codicibus ejusmodi concessionis indicium nullum repertum est, exemplum rescripti alias impetrati, in quo dies, mensis, et annus concessionis adnotatus sit ad nos mittere ne gravere, ut ad illius normam indulgentiarum renovationem obtinere valeamus. Eo exemplo eo magis indigemus, quod in tua istius diœcesis relatione nobis significaveris, quibus conditionibus indulgentiæ acquirantur, non dissimulans ab aliquibus hujusmodi pii exercitii praxim fuisse improbatam. Visum est etiam nobis circuitiones quasdam, nisi probabiles earum causæ afferantur, posse jure meritoque notari ; præsertim cum non modo pedibus, sed cruribus etiam nudis fieri in more sit positum ; quod si a fidelibus utrinsque sexus fiat, timendum est ne aliquod inde scandalum oriatur. . . . Quod si forte in ista Sti. Patritii peregrinatione ejusmodi abusus irrepserit, tuæ partes erunt omni studio ac contentione eosdem eliminare ne mala potius quam bona a tali peregrinatione exoriantur.*" . . . .*

---

*Father Luke Concanen, to whom reference is made in this rescript, was the first Bishop of New York. When in Rome he acted as agent to the Irish bishops, and lived in the Dominican convent attached to the Church of *Santa Maria sopra Minerva*. It is worthy of note that this is the titular church of his successor, Cardinal M'Closkey, the first Cardinal in the United States.

This document has also the signature of *Dominicus Archiepus. Myran., Secretarius.*

From the foregoing rescript we can understand with what vigilance the authorities in Rome had watched over this sanctuary, and how the report (probably gratuitous and groundless) which had reached them of the pilgrims here making the circuits of the "beds" on their bare knees, had been inquired after and corrected. When Dr. Murphy gave the required information to the Sacred Office, the indulgences postulated for were granted ; and when the same bishop again applied for their renewal in 1814, they were also accorded, as we can infer from the form of postulation on this head, presented to the Holy Father in 1870, a copy of which, together with a copy of the Papal Indult, will be found in this work.

In the year 1813 the church built by Father O'Doherty in 1763 was taken down, and a new church, also called St. Mary's, erected a little to the east of it by the Very Rev. Patrick Bellew, then Prior, afterwards parish priest of Monaghan and Dean of Clogher. In 1835 the Rev. Prior Moyna enlarged this church by the erection of an aisle, the contractor for the improvements then effected being the late Daniel Campbell, builder, Pettigo. This church underwent additional repairs in 1860 ; and in 1870 it was found necessary to have it taken down entirely, when it was replaced by a very substantial and handsome Gothic edifice, through the exertions of the Rev. James M'Kenna, P.P. (who has done so much in erecting, enlarging, and repairing the buildings on Station Island), and solely with the aid of the voluntary contri-

butions of the pilgrims. St. Mary's new church was
dedicated in August, 1870, the year in which it was
erected, by the Most Rev. Dr. Donnelly. To those who
have admired this pretty little church, with the campanile
and bell hard by, erected at the same time, it will afford
surprise to learn that all cost little over £500. In this
church a number of confessionals are located, where the
officiating priests labour most of the day in the sacred
and sublime work of reconciling sinners to God. To this
sacred use and purpose the church is, I may say, entirely
devoted. The presbytery, which was a substantially-
built and commodious house, was erected by Prior
Bellew in 1816. It was afterwards, in 1860, considerably
remodelled internally ; and finally, in 1864 it was in great
part rebuilt by the Rev. James M'Kenna, at the cost of
£164.

If it be a mark of the sanctity of a place to be made the
constant object of attack by heretical and infidel writers,
then surely must Lough Derg, independent of any other
reason, be regarded as very holy, inasmuch as never yet
was there an institution more bitterly and more per-
sistently assailed than this pilgrimage. Misrepresentation,
calumny, invective, ridicule, and all the other artifices of
the enemies of our holy religion, have been all employed
against this exercise of Catholic piety. Besides the many
charges brought against it, all of which might with equal
force be directed against any Catholic practice or place
of Catholic worship throughout the world, Richardson,
and others after him, have devised a new and ingenious
objection, showing the loss of time and the waste of

money, both to the individual and to the State, by the toleration of this pilgrimage—an objection which clearly demonstrates with what spirit the enemies of pilgrimages are inspired—by making, forsooth, temporal interests of more paramount importance than those spiritual interests which the pious pilgrim so anxiously labours to compass !

During the present century the sanctuary was resorted to by writers of this class, whose object was to gratify the prejudices of the enemies of our holy religion by representing in the darkest colours this time-honoured retreat. Principal amongst this class stand Cæsar Otway and his *protégé*, Carleton. William Carleton, the novelist, having abandoned the faith of his fathers for the sake of lucre, devoted his distempered genius to ridicule and malign the faith in which he was baptized, and the religious practices of his countrymen. Born in the townland of Kilnahussogue, parish of Clogher, in 1795, he came to Lough Derg about 1820, as if on pilgrimage. Soon after he renounced his faith, he wrote a most ludicrous and absurd story, in which he himself figures as the *Lough Derg Pilgrim*. Another writer, Mr. Inglis, takes a very ultra-Protestant view of the pilgrimage in his *Journey throughout Ireland*, in 1834. In the same strain writes Philip Dixon Hardy, in his *Holy Wells of Ireland* (Dublin, 1836), who by his pencil not less than by his pen has left behind him a very poor caricature of the place. Wright's *St. Patrick's Purgatory* (London, 1844) is a tissue of bigotry from beginning to end.

Amongst the accounts of this pilgrimage written by Protestants, the notice of it in *Household Words* of

October, 1852, is an honourable exception.   At first it
was thought that Charles Dickens had been the writer of
this notice, and that he visited the island in person. The
authorship of the article is, however, now generally
ascribed to Allingham, the poet. This account of the
pilgrimage was very impartial and favourable ; it praised
Prior Moyna's lectures as being learned and practical,
and bestowed a fitting eulogium on the deep piety and
devotion of the pilgrims.

In the year 1829 Father Bellew was Prior for the last
time. After him came Father Boylan, who held the
office for two years. He afterwards became P.P. of
Enniskillen and Dean of Clogher. He was succeeded as
Prior of Lough Derg by the Rev. Patrick Moyna, who
continued in this office for about twenty-nine years. The
present venerated Prior, Very Rev. Edward Canon
M'Kenna, P.P., Dromore, has filled the position, with
but little interruption, since the death of Father Moyna
in 1860.   Thus it will be seen that the Priors of Lough
Derg, as a rule, were very long-lived, and that they were
favoured with a lengthened term of office.

During the present century many illustrious pilgrims
and visitors have been at Lough Derg. Foremost
amongst these may be recorded the names of the following
prelates—Dr. Patrick M'Gettigan, Bishop of Raphoe ;
Dr. M'Loughlin, Bishop of Derry ; Dr. Kilduff, Bishop
of Ardagh ; the Most Rev. Daniel M'Gettigan, now Lord
Primate ; and, in addition, the Bishops of Clogher, in
which diocese the sanctuary is situated. Besides these
distinguished ecclesiastics, a great many of the clergy of

Ireland, and not a few from other countries also, have
made during this century pilgrimage to Lough Derg—
some even selecting it for the annual ecclesiastical retreat.
Members of the religious orders throughout Ireland visit
this sanctuary time after time, and express the greatest
admiration not only at the earnest piety and penitential
spirit manifested by the pilgrims, but also at the order,
regularity, and efficiency with which the devotional exercises of the station are conducted. It will interest the
readers to learn that in 1875 Father Dalgairns, who,
under God, was instrumental in converting the Marquis
of Ripon, came on a visit to Lough Derg, and there
caused prayers to be offered up for the conversion of a
distinguished statesman, whose name he did not commu-
nicate, but which was soon after fully made known by
the event.

The bright example of penance and humility, as shown
by these pious ecclesiastics, who passed through the
curriculum of this station, gave great edification to the
lay pilgrims, and conduced to swell the stream of pilgrims
towards this venerable shrine. During the first half of
the present century the number of pilgrims to Lough
Derg each year was much in excess of the numbers since
attending. From the year 1800 down to 1824 the average
yearly number was about 10,000. In 1824, I have it
from the oldest pilgrim to this sanctuary, Mr. Edward
Nicholson, architect and engineer, Manchester, that, on
the occasion of his first visit in that year, there were
1,100 pilgrims on the same night keeping vigil in
" Prison " Chapel. This Mr. Nicholson was a disciple

and most intimate friend of the late Mr. Pugin; and having made it a regular custom to spend his annual holidays in Ireland, he never failed, during these intervals of relaxation, to visit the sanctuary of Lough Derg, of which he has proved himself a constant friend and benefactor. From this and other sources we infer that in 1824 the number of pilgrims must have been in excess of 15,000. In 1834 Mr. Inglis tells us that the number of arrivals must have reached 19,000. In the beginning of the famine years (1846) there arrived in a single day the extraordinary number of 1,300 pilgrims, the greatest number, it is said, that, during this century, came to Lough Derg in one day; and we learn that during this year the total number of arrivals could not have been much under 30,000. During these seasons from twelve to fifteen priests were engaged in hearing the confessions of the pilgrims and attending to the other station duties.

Since 1846 there has been a gradual decline in the number of arrivals each year down to 1870. For this falling off in point of numbers various reasons may be assigned. Foremost amongst these is the famine of '47, and the consequent depopulation of our country by emigration and extirpation; also the facilities of missions and retreats, which have of late multiplied to such a degree throughout Ireland; and, perhaps too, the lessened fervour of the faithful. The closing of the station in 1860, while repairs were being made on the island, the building of St. Mary's in 1870, and further building and repairs during the season of 1878, may have had some effect in diminishing the number of pilgrims of late years.

Beginning with 1870, the numbers are each year steadily increasing. Since then between three and four thousand pilgrims annually perform the station here. Of these the great majority are Irish, or of Irish parentage. A great many of them come from America, many from England and Scotland, and not a few from Australia, New Zealand, and the other distant colonies—in a word, from wherever the exiled Celt has found a foothold. The Island of Lough Derg would seem to be the common meeting-place of the Irish race, whither they journey from the most distant parts to keep vigil, to fast and pray at the " Holy Island," even as the Jews were wont to journey at fixed seasons towards their holy city of Jerusalem. Occasionally pilgrims of foreign nationalities kneel before this sanctuary, and pour out their prayers in strange tongues. But it is of the faithful Irish race the pilgrimage is almost wholly composed, who will here be met with, not only from all parts of Ireland, but from many foreign places as well. And though the devotions are now conducted in the English language, yet before this shrine many a prayer is still offered up in " the sweet-tongued language of the Gael."

Instances are numerous of persons who, drawn by the holy attractions of the place, repeat the pilgrimage year after year. Mr. Nicholson, who may justly be styled the patriarch of the pilgrims, has been here on pilgrimage for the last fifty-four years, with very few exceptions. A worthy Belfast-man, Mr. Henry, in company with an organised party of pilgrims from Belfast, has been here close on fifty seasons. Many others have been here

twenty or thirty times ; and, out of the aggregate number
each season, it is true to say that about one-third of the
number is composed of pilgrims who have been previously
to the island.   The same as in former years, the majority
of the pilgrims still consists of men ; while persons of
every class and age and condition in life may be here
observed, performing with the greatest humility and piety
the devotional exercises of the pilgrimage.   It is a
remarkable fact that all those, who have once made the
pilgrimage, have left the island with sorrowful regret, and
with the most lively hope of returning some other season,
and of tasting again those sweet pleasures of soul which
the pilgrimage, albeit the apparent severity of its exercises, occasions.   The sorrow of the pilgrims at parting
from the island is faithfully depicted in the following ode,
which is so full of pathos, and sung to a sweet and
plaintive air :—

FAREWELL HYMN TO LOUGH DERG.

" Oh ! fare thee well, Lough Derg,
    Shall I ever see you more ?
My heart is filled with sorrow
    To leave thy sainted shore.
Until life's days have passed away,
    No pleasures can beguile
My thoughts from often turning
    Back to thy sacred isle.

II.

" Saint Patrick was its founder,
    At Heaven's express command,
To cleanse away the sinful stains
    Of his own loved Ireland ;

In hopes by prayer and penance here
   God's mercy to secure,
Lest punishments hereafter
   For them we may endure.

III.

" He blessed with sweet devotion
   This penitential isle ;
He chose as its director
   St. Dabheoc, without guile ;
While hosts of saints and hermits here
   True happiness did find,
By leaving home and worldly joys
   And kindred all behind.

IV.

" Throughout each station season,
   From every distant clime,
The children of St. Patrick
   Frequent this holy shrine.
Each pilgrim here is edified
   With piety sincere,
And it's here each soul is purified
   By penances severe.

V.

" But when the Holy Island
   Is fading out of view,
With tears the grateful pilgrims
   To it they bid adieu ;
Saying, ' May its name still spread abroad,
   Its fame grow greater still,
Its Patron Saint still honour'd be,
   And crowds its cloisters fill.'

VI.

"So fare you well, Lough Derg;
    Shall I ever see you more?
My heart is filled with sorrow
    To leave thy sainted shore.
Until life's days have passed away,
    With pleasure shall I dwell
On the happy days I spent with you,
    Lough Derg, fare thee well!"

Formerly this was chanted at the departure of each boat from the island, by a person who volunteered her services for that purpose; but latterly it has been discontinued, and has become almost quite forgotten, like many other glorious memories of this ancient retreat.

CHAPTER XVII.

ROUTES TO LOUGH DERG — ROAD FROM PETTIGO —
THOUGHTS ON NEARING THE LAKE—LITHOGRAPHIC
VIEWS OF THE ISLAND—THE STATION SEASON—THE
AUTHORIZED RELIGIOUS EXERCISES OF THE PILGRIMAGE
—EXPLANATORY OBSERVATIONS ON THE "EXERCISES"—
MOST REV. DR. DONNELLY PETITIONS THE HOLY SEE FOR
INDULGENCES—COPY OF THE PAPAL INDULT.

FORMERLY a pilgrimage to Lough Derg must have been attended with much hardship and inconvenience, when we consider that pilgrims travelled, in many cases barefoot, from the most remote parts of the kingdom. Considering, however, the facilities of travelling which we enjoy at the present day, the journey is now regarded as little more than a pleasant excursion trip. Good roads lead towards the lake, though, we regret to say, not to its shore ; a line of railway runs pretty close to it ; well-appointed cars in connection with each train ply between the lake and railway ; in a word, pilgrims have now-a-days little to complain of from fatigue or inconvenience, till they are landed on the island of Lough Derg.

There are three routes by which pilgrims reach Lough Derg. The first of these starts from the town of Donegal, and, after proceeding for about five miles along a good

N

county road, it enters on a mountain track leading in a direct line towards the lake, passing along the side of Augh-Keen Mountain, and reaching the lake at a head-land close to Saints' Island. By this route come many of the sons and daughters of old Tyrconnell ; while others of them, less observant of the ancient usage, and prefer-ring the more easy mode of travelling by car, take the roundabout way by Pettigo. Some years since a project was in contemplation of running a boat on certain days to the mouth of the River Fluchlynn, for the greater con-venience of the Donegal pilgrims. This would be to them a saving of about three miles across a difficult stretch of moorland, and would make the journey from Donegal to the lake only about six miles. Should the number of arrivals warrant it, I see no reason why this project may not hereafter be put in operation.

The second route leads from Castlederg, past Killeter, on through the district of Aughayarran, and terminates at the "cabin," or ferryhouse. This route leads by a very good road till within view of the lake, when (the same as on the previous route) the pilgrim has to tread the re-mainder of the way over a well-beaten mountain track. Very many pilgrims from the counties of Derry, Tyrone, and part of Donegal come by this way ; though many others prefer travelling from Castlederg to Pettigo by car.

The third and principal way is that from Pettigo. All the pilgrims, who come by train or car, proceed to the lake by this route. Nor will it be out of place here to state that "Lough Derg return tickets" available for return within fourteen days, and at a reduced rate of fare, are furnished to pilgrims at the principal stations of the different lines and branches of the Great Northern Railway. On the arrival of each train at Pettigo, there are cars in waiting to convey the pilgrims to the lake. Those who prefer remaining over night in Pettigo will find there good hotel and inn accommodation, and will meet with, on all sides, kindness and attention from the inhabitants. The same may be said of the accommodation, courtesy, and civility to be experienced both in Donegal and Castlederg. From the map of the lake and its surroundings, which we append to this work, the reader will be able to comprehend these three routes to Lough Derg, with the respective distances of these towns from the lake.

A good road leads from Pettigo in the direction of Lough Derg; but, when within about half a mile from the lake (through whose fault I do not inquire, though it certainly redounds but little to the credit either of the local magnates, or of the Donegal Grand Jury), the road stops short at the mountain side, and the pilgrim has to enter on a boggy path, which in wet weather baffles description. And yet these pilgrims pay their share of county cess, and the island itself is also assessed! And, again, these pilgrims pay a tax of eightpence each to the lord of the soil for permission to cross the haunts of the hare and moorfowl, and thence to be ferried to Station Island; and for these no road has been hitherto allowed, even at the public expense! Verily might we here moralize with Burns on " man's inhumanity to man ;" but we will rest content with asking, if it were the merest Protestant conventicle of which there was question, would this condition of things, think you, be allowed to continue for a single day ? At length, I understand, an effort has been made to have this track converted into a good county road, and thus the old reproach will be finally got rid of.

A portion of the mountain adjoining this track has been planted with firs in 1847, which, together with some of the islands planted the same year, gives a pleasing variety to the otherwise wild scenery of this locality; and where eagles and wild geese (as Richardson states) used to frequent about a century ago, the sweet notes of feathered songsters of the grove may now be heard.

The feelings of the pilgrim, when a sudden turn in the road brings him within full view of the lake and of Station Island, may better be imagined than described. On reaching the "cabin," as the ferryhouse is commonly called, may be witnessed the spectacle referred to by Mr. Inglis, a writer by no means friendly to the pilgrimage :—" As I descended towards the shore of the lake, I could see that the island was entirely covered with persons, and on the bank I found upwards of two hundred pilgrims waiting to be ferried over. They were generally respectably dressed; some were sitting, some lying on the grass ; some, more impatient, were standing close to the water, waiting the arrival of the ferryboat ; and some, more impatient still, had been warmed into devotion by the distant view of the holy place, and were already on their knees."

The large pilgrim's boat is appropriately called the "St. Patrick ;" it is manned by steady and experienced boatmen, and is capable of accommodating about sixty pilgrims.

A smaller boat is called the " St. Brigid," and another the "St. Columba." Any of these can make the passage from the ferryhouse to the island—distance something under a statute mile—in ten or fifteen minutes. The pilgrims will receive strict attention from the ferryman, Mr. Patrick Flood, than whom a more competent person for that responsible position could hardly be desired.

When the pilgrims arrive on the island, they proceed to one or other of the lodging-houses, which are six in number, and there they divest themselves of shoes and hats, in order to perform the station both barefoot and bareheaded.

Station Island is in length 126 yards; in the broadest place 45, and in the narrowest 22 yards in width. In the summer of 1871, Mr. Edward Nicholson, of Manchester, obtained permission to take a sketch of the island, and to have, at his own expense, lithographic printings of it struck off. This work was effected in 1873 by the firm of Mac-Gregor and Company, Manchester. The lithographs, together with the lithographic blocks, were presented by Mr. Nicholson to the bishop of the diocese, the Most Rev. Dr. Donnelly, for the use of the island. It is a very beautiful work of art, and a number of copies of it are exposed for sale each season on the island. This sketch, which is furnished with a reference table in the margin, will be found invaluable as a map, as a guide, and as a picture of Station Island. It clearly represents the two churches on the island, St. Patrick's and St. Mary's, the campanile, St. Patrick's cross, the penitential beds, or oratories, dedicated to Saints Dabheoc, Molaise Columba,

Catherine, Brendan, and Brigid; the stations at the water,
the presbytery, the boarding-house, and the boat-quay.
Even the solitary sycamore tree, which formerly served the
purposes of a belfry, and which is the only tree or shrub
on the island,* is accurately represented on this drawing.
Mr. Wakeman, of Enniskillen, has also published a beautiful lithographic view of the lake and island, with the pilgrims' boat on its passage : from this our frontispiece
illustration for this work has been taken.

The station season at Lough Derg formerly extended
from June the 1st till the 15th of August. In 1869, however, it was limited from 1st July till the 15th of August,
which is still the period during which the island is open
for pilgrimage. With the increase in the number of pilgrims it may, we hope, be soon rendered advisable to
recur to the old station period.

We have already seen that the pilgrimage, according to
modern custom, lasts for three days, though some continue
their station for six, and even for nine days. It is customary
for the pilgrims to arrive fasting, and to perform at least
one station before taking food; hence it is that most of the
pilgrims arrive in the earlier part of the day. Should the
pilgrim not arrive fasting, this will necessitate his remaining an additional night on the island, as he cannot com-
mence the station till the next day. During the pilgrimage
three stations are performed each day. For the conve-

---

* That there were a number of trees on the island during the last
century, where the presbytery now stands, appears from the plate of
the island given in Ledwich's *Antiquities of Ireland.*

nience and guidance of the pilgrims a large number of copies of the authorised devotional exercises of this pilgrimage were printed in the summer of 1876, and each pilgrim can obtain a copy at the island, with the aid of which he will have little difficulty in going through the routine of the station exercises. I here insert a copy of these exercises.

DEVOTIONAL EXERCISES OF THE PILGRIMAGE OF LOUGH DERG.

" Unless you shall do penance, you shall all likewise perish." Luke, c. xiii., v. 3.

"The station commences with a visit to the Blessed Sacrament in St. Patrick's Church.

"The pilgrim then proceeds to 'St. Patrick's Cross,' near the same church, and kneeling, repeats there one Pater, one Ave, and Creed.

"Next he goes to 'St. Brigid's Cross,' where kneeling, he recites three Paters, three Aves, and one Creed. Then standing with his back to the Cross, and outstretched arms, he thrice renounces the Devil, the World, and the Flesh.

"He then makes seven circuits of St. Patrick's Church, repeating in each circuit one decade of the Rosary, and adding a Creed to the last decade.

"He next proceeds to the Penitential Cell or Bed, nearest to St. Mary's Church, called St. Brigid's Bed, and says three Paters, three Aves, and one Creed, whilst thrice making the circuit of this Bed on the ouside. The same prayers are repeated while kneeling outside the enrance of the Bed, the same repeated while making three circuits of it on the inside, and the same prayers are repeated while kneeling at the cross inside the Bed.

"The same penitential exercises are performed successively at St. Brendan's Bed, St. Catherine's and St. Columba's.

"Around the large Penitential Bed nine circuits are then made on the outside, while repeating nine Paters, nine Aves, and one Creed.

The pilgrim then kneels at the first entrance of this Bed, and recites three Paters, three Aves, and one Creed. He next repeats three Paters, three Aves, and one Creed, while making the inside circuit of it ; and again, three Paters, three Aves, and a Creed, kneeling in the centre. He now proceeds to the second entrance of this Bed (which entrance is the one nearer to St. Patrick's Church), and kneeling, recites three Paters, three Aves, and one Creed.   The same prayers are recited whilst making the inner circuit of it, and the same kneeling in the centre.

"The pilgrim now goes to the water's edge, where five Paters, five Aves, and one Creed are repeated standing, and the same prayers kneeling.

" After this he returns to St. Patrick's Cross, from which he had first set out, and here the station is concluded by saying on his knees one Pater, one Ave, and one Creed.

"Three stations with the foregoing prayers are performed each day, each station being usually followed by five decades of the Rosary of the Blessed Virgin.

" The pilgrim enters ' Prison ' on the evening of the first day, and there he makes the stations for the second day by reciting the prayers of each station as already given.

" On the second day of the pilgrimage each one goes to confession, and on the morning of the third day to Holy Communion.

" In addition to the foregoing exercises, the pilgrim assists each day at morning prayer, Mass, meditation, visit to the Blessed Sacrament, spiritual reading, evening prayer, sermon, and benediction with the Blessed Sacrament.

"Any information regarding the fast, &c., may be easily obtained on the island.

"The station opens each year on the 1st of July, and closes on the 15th of August, the festival of the Assumption of the Blessed Virgin."

According to the Papal Indult (a copy of which is inserted in this chapter) it is required, in order to gain the indulgence attached to this pilgrimage, to offer up prayers on this island for the propagation of the Faith and according to the Pope's intention. No particular prayers are enjoined, but Bouvier, *Traite des Indulgences* (p. 73), says that in such a case five Paters and Aves will suffice, or one of the litanies or some psalms, or two decades of the rosary, &c.

The better to enable pilgrims to understand how to get through with their station, I shall here add some explanatory information.

The pilgrim enters " prison " (*i.e.*, St. Patrick's Church, so called because it serves the purpose of the ancient purgatorial cave) the first evening after he commences his station, and remains there till next morning. During the night "in prison" strict vigil is kept ; the stations for the following day are gone through, some person well acquainted with the routine of the exercises directing the attention of those present to the different beds or oratories, &c.; and the intervals of the night are occupied with reciting rosaries, going round the stations of the Cross, &c.

At six o'clock, at latest, each morning, morning prayer commences in St. Patrick's Church, followed by the community Mass. At twelve o'clock, noon, there is a visit to the Blessed Sacrament in St. Patrick's Church, followed by a spiritual lecture. At six o'clock each evening the bell summons the pilgrims to evening prayer in the same church, after which a sermon is preached, and this is followed by benediction with the Blessed Sacrament. The religious discourses here delivered are of the most practical kind, are well calculated to awaken in the hearts of the pil-

grims a sense of the eternal truths and of their religious
obligations, and are of great aid and benefit to the pilgrims in preparing for confession and Holy Communion.

Moving round the churches and saints' beds (which is
a distinctive feature in this pilgrimage, which is of very
great antiquity, and which, though not peculiar to Ireland,
was formerly in this country a very common form of penance and devotion) is clearly explained in the "Exercises"
given above.   These beds are the oldest buildings at present on Station Island, they are pretty closely grouped
together, and very probably they have received no material
alteration for the last three hundred years, when they were
first constructed here after the model of the little oratories
on Saints' Island.   Four of these beds are surrounded by
a low circular wall, not over one foot in height ; while the
walls round two others are about three feet high.   They
do not exceed ten or eleven feet in diameter, with the exception of St. Molaise's Bed, which is sixteen feet in
diameter.   A small gap in the circular wall forms an entrance to each of these beds, the inner space is paved with
stones or formed of the bare rock, worn smooth by the
feet of pilgrims for so many generations; and in the centre
of each bed stands a crucifix, having underneath the name
of the saint to whom the bed is dedicated.   Three of
these bronze crucifixes inscribed respectively "St. Patrick,"
" St. Brigid," and " St. Columbkille," were presented to
the island by the late John Donegan, jeweller, Dublin ;
while the remaining three crucifixes were ordered from
Munich by Mr. Edward Nicholson, of Manchester, and
presented to the island during the present year.

A large stone at the verge of the lake, and partly sub-
mersed in water, is called Leᴀc nᴀ mbonn (which signifies
the broad stone under the feet), and here the station at
the water is performed, as it is popularly credited that St.
Patrick and the other saints of this retreat used here to
pray and to suffer penance.

The fast from immemorial custom consists of one meal
of meagre food each day ; but wherever any just cause
exists for a relaxation in this, or in any other of the penitential austerities of the place, the prior and the other confessors on the island, will afford every reasonable concession, according to each particular case. To the credit,
however, of the genuine faith and piety of the Irish people
be it said, that the great majority of the pilgrims cheer-
fully undergo all the austerities of this pilgrimage, wisely
considering a three days' mortification and penance as but
light and easy in comparison to the temporal punishment
due to sin.

On the second day of the pilgrimage, each pilgrim goes
to confession in St. Mary's Church, and if he should live
a considerable distance from the lake, he usually gets permission from his confessor to perform one or two of the
stations for the following day, in order to permit him to
leave the island at an earlier hour. On the third day Holy
Communion is received, the nine stations are completed,
the prior's blessing is obtained, and the pilgrim leaves for
home, unless he wishes to prolong his stay for six or nine
days. The sum of about three shillings will cover the ex-
penses of each pilgrim while on the island, and this includes
the tribute paid to the ferryman, and also the offering paid

by each pilgrim towards the support of the clergy ministering to the pilgrims, and to defray the other incidental
expenditure of the place.

Pilgrims are forbidden, by a special rule, the use of
intoxicating drinks on the island, or within three miles of
it; and they are also forbidden to carry away with them
any pebbles or water from the lake, lest they should attach
to these things any undue value.

Our readers will be able to form some idea of the piety
and devotion practised at this holy retreat, when we tell
them that a station at present consists, besides the visit
to the Blessed Sacrament, of 97 Paters, 160 Aves, and
29 Creeds ; that three of these stations are performed each
day; and that at the end of each day's stations five
decades of the Rosary of the Blessed Virgin are said.
There are some who perform the station according to the
old practice (the ritual of the pilgrimage having undergone some mitigation in modern times), and in their case
11 Paters, 11 Aves, 3 Creeds, and 10 decades of the
Rosary are said, in addition to the above.   Over and
above this, the pilgrim assists at Mass, morning and
evening prayer, meditations, the *Angelus* three times daily,
sermons and benediction with the Blessed Sacrament.   It
will thus be seen that the time of the pilgrims, while on
the island, is fully occupied, and that there is no room
here for worldly or idle conversations.

The throng of pilgrims greatly increases towards the
festival of the Assumption, when the station closes ; and
we here venture to suggest that if the pilgrims should
come in greater numbers at an early part of the station

season, they would very much consult for their own com. fort and accommodation.

We have already seen that this venerable sanctuary was greatly cherished by several of the Roman Pontiffs, and that they enriched it with indulgences, which, in latter ages, were granted anew after the lapse of every fifteen years. The last renewal of this plenary indulgence was granted on the 26th of June, 1870, by the late Holy Father, Pope Pius IX., of holy memory. Through the kindness of the venerated Bishop of Clogher, the Most Rev. Dr. Donnelly, I am enabled to enrich the pages of this work with copies of the *Postulatio*, and also of the Papal Indult itself.

The form of postulation is written in Italian, and is countersigned, " D. B. Smith. J—— 25, 1870."

This *Postulatio* is as follows :—

" BEATISSIMO PADRE,

" Giacomo Donnelly, Vescovo di Clogher, in Irlanda, religio-samente espone alla Santita Vostra quanto seque.

" Nella sua diocesi avvi un santuario detto il Purgatorio di S. Patrizio, frequentato dai divoti non solo d'Irlanda, ma d'Inghilterra e di Scozia ; ogni pellegrino passa almeno tre giorni in detto santuario in pii esercizi, e frequenza dei sacramenti della Confessione ed Eucaristia, secondo la direzione dei preti secolari, che diriggono quel luogo : di esso parla ancora Benedetto XIII., nel Sermone 13, de Purgatorio ; egle storici dicono che un tal pelegrinaggio sia stato instituito da S. Patrizio stesso. Benche nel tempo della perse-cuzione dei Protestanti si adoperasse ogni sforzo per rovinar detto santuario, pure non vi si vinsci ; ed esso dura ancora con immenso vantaggio della salute spirituale dei prossimi, e religione Cattolica.

" Secondo il *Relatio Status* fatto nel 1814 da Monsigr. Murphy,

Vescovo di Clogher la S. Sede aveva concessa una indulgenza alla visita del Purgatorio di S. Patrizio.

"Quindi S. Oratore supplica la sanctita vostra degnarsi di accordare l'indulgenza plenaria, applicabile alle anime del purgatorio, a tutti i fideli, che premetti i sancti sacramenti della Confessione e Communione visita un detto santuario, e cio *toties quoties* ripeteranno dette prattiche della SS. Communione durante gli esercizi che ecc."

The following may be regarded as a pretty accurate translation of the foregoing document :—

"MOST HOLY FATHER,

"James Donnelly, Bishop of Clogher, in Ireland, respectfully submits to your Holiness what follows.

"In his diocese he has a sanctuary called St. Patrick's Purgatory, which is frequented by the devout not only of Ireland, but from England and Scotland also. Each pilgrim spends at least three days at the said sanctuary in pious exercises, and frequentation of the sacraments of Confession and the Eucharist, under the direction of the secular priests, who have charge of the place. Of it, likewise, Benedict XIII. speaks in the 13th Sermon on Purgatory. Historians say that such a pilgrimage was established by the said St. Patrick. And although at the time of the persecution by the Protestants, every effort was made to destroy the said sanctuary, yet they could not destroy it ; and it still subsists with immense advantage to the spiritual welfare of the surrounding people, and to the Catholic religion.

"According to the *Relatio Status*, made in 1814 by Dr. Murphy, Bishop of Clogher, the Holy See had attached an indulgence to the visit of the Purgatory of St. Patrick.

"Hence Petitioner begs that your Holiness will be pleased to grant a plenary indulgence, applicable to the souls in Purgatory, to all the faithful who shall have previously received the Holy Sacraments of Confession and Communion, and visited the said sanctuary, and who repeat *toties quoties* the aforesaid practice of Holy Communion during the exercises," &c., &c.

The following is a copy of the Papal Indult, granting the prayer of the above petition by according a plenary indulgence to this pilgrimage :—

" Ex audientia SSimi, die 26 Junii, 1870.

" SSimus D. N. Pius Divina Providentia PP. IX. referente me infra-scripto S. C. de Propaganda Fide Secretario, benigne prorogavit Indulgentiam Plenariam lucrandam ab omnibus Christi fidelibus, qui confessi ac sacra Eucharistia refecti prædictam capellam vulgo Purgatorium S. Patritii visitaverint, ibique per aliquod temporis spatium pias ad Deum fuderint preces pro S. Fidei propagatione, et juxta summi Pontificis intentionem.

" Dat. Romæ ex æd. dic. S. C. die et anno ut supra.

" Gratis sine ulla solutione quocumque titulo.

" JOANNES SIMEONI, Secretarius."

This Indult may be translated as follows :—

" From an audience of His Holiness, on the 26th day of June, 1870.

" Our Most Holy Father Pius IX., by Divine Providence Pope, at the representation of me, the undersigned Secretary of the Sacred Congregation *de Propaganda Fide*, has graciously prolonged the concession of a plenary indulgence to be gained by all the faithful, who, having confessed and being nourished by the Holy Eucharist, shall have visited the above-mentioned sanctuary, commonly called the Purgatory of St. Patrick, and there, during some space of time, shall have offered up pious prayers to God for the propagation of our holy faith, and according to the intention of the Sovereign Pontiff.

" Given at Rome, from the Office of said Sacred Congregation, on the date and year above named.

" *Gratis*, without any payment under whatever title.

" JOHN SIMEONI, Secretary."

From the foregoing Indult it will be seen that the indulgences accorded to this pilgrimage are given for an indefinite period, and consequently they may be understood to continue annexed to the pilgrimage until withdrawn by the Holy See.

To the pious pilgrim to Lough Derg, it cannot but be a source of the most heartfelt satisfaction to read the above Indult, which shall ever be regarded as the title-deed of the sanctity of this penitential retreat, and as the endowment of it with spiritual graces by a Pontiff, whose career was so glorious, and who loved the Irish race so much because of their constant faith and fervent piety.

CHAPTER XVIII.

THE HEALTHFUL CLIMATE OF LOUGH DERG—PECULIAR
EFFICACY OF THE EXERCISES OF THIS STATION—THE JOY
AND PEACE EXPERIENCED IN THIS PILGRIMAGE—BENE-
FACTORS OF THIS TRULY CATHOLIC CHARITY—CON-
CLUDING REMARKS.

VISITORS to Lough Derg speak in the highest praise of the salubrious quality of its climate. Nor is this to be wondered at; for, situated as it is within about four miles, in a direct line, from Donegal Bay, it enjoys the advantage of the sea air, tempered by the mountain breezes; so that during the dry, warm days of summer the atmosphere of Lough Derg is the most healthful, bracing, and invigorating perhaps of any other locality in Ireland. And to this circumstance may be, to a great extent, ascribed the almost total immunity from mortality which the island has enjoyed; for the oldest inhabitants of the place can only remember one or two deaths to have occurred here out of such crowds of pilgrims, many of whom were old and feeble persons, who travelled very long journeys to the island, and there performed the different exercises in all their rigour. It is now nearly forty years since the last death occurred on the island; and

O

that was in the case of an aged woman, who was interred in the cemetery of the pilgrimage on Saints' Island, and whose funeral was accompanied to her last resting-place by the pilgrims then "on station." So genial is the atmosphere of the locality, that few are heard to complain of the slightest indisposition while they remain here ; and if this be owing in some part to the healthful climate of the place, it cannot be denied that the practice of penance and mortification here observed has a great deal to do with this happy state of things; the practice of mortification not only being of salutary advantage to the soul, but contributing, likewise, towards the health of the body.

It is a remarkable fact, upon which many comment, that the devotional exercises of this pilgrimage have a wonderful efficacy in securing the necessary dispositions for worthily receiving the sacraments of Penance and Holy Communion. Hence it is that many persons, after having attended missions and retreats elsewhere (such persons regarding missions as only a preparatory course for properly entering on this pilgrimage), come here in order to secure that interior happiness which its exercises are so calculated to produce. Nor are there wanting many and convincing reasons to show the peculiar efficacy of these exercises. In the first place, that crucial test of the sanctity of a place, the *nonne cor nostrum ardens erat in nobis*, here forces itself on the mind. One feels in this place, as it were instinctively, that he walks upon holy ground; that here the prayer blessed by penance is certain of being heard ; that here the soul is allowed close converse with God ; that here Heaven bestows its choicest blessings, and that here God enriches the pious pilgrims with copious graces.

Besides, every penitential exercise here practised increases in the soul veneration for the sanctity of the place, coupled with love and reverence for God—the Author of all sanctity. At the very outset of the station, the pilgrim divests himself of his shoes, out of respect for the sanctity of the place, through a spirit of penance, and in conformity with the admonition given by God to Moses—"Come not nigh hither ; put off the shoes from thy feet, for the place whereon thou standest is holy ground" (Exod., c. iii., v. 5). In addition to this, the men wear neither hat nor cap while on the island.

Again, are not the observances of fasting, vigil, and prayer, as here observed, in direct keeping with the constant teaching and precepts of our Blessed Saviour? And where, may I ask, are these salutary precepts so faithfully followed as on the holy island of Lough Derg? Need we wonder, then, that they are such powerful helps in disposing the pilgrims for a worthy reception of the sacraments? Next, walking round the churches and saints' beds, over the uneven surface of the rock, rough stones, water gravel, &c., does it not convey the very idea of pilgrimage, and suggest very forcibly man's mortal pilgrimage through the desert places of this world—of this "vale of tears?" In going round the saints' beds we are reminded of the penitential and mortified lives led by those great servants of God, who, within these little cells, or in others of similar construction at this hallowed retreat, are said to have done penance during the day, and to have reposed their weary limbs during the night. Going through these stations also reminds the pilgrims of that infinitely more painful journey, the way of the Cross, along which our Blessed Lord bore the heavy weight of the Cross, for our sake, up the rugged hill of Calvary. And when the pilgrim stands with outstretched arms in front of the cross, set in the eastern wall of St. Patrick's Church, does he not thereby signify that, having renounced the devil, the world, and the flesh, he is prepared to take up his cross and follow in the footsteps of his Divine Master?

By going into " prison," or the fast-cave, or sepulchre, as it is differently named, the pilgrim is reminded that he is now dead to the world and its vanities ; and that having buried, so to say, his past transgressions, he may rise again to the supernatural life of grace, or to a higher degree of perfection. The ablution usually performed after leaving " prison," is expressive of the interior cleansing which the penitential works of the station and the reception of the sacraments operate in the soul of the pilgrim.

The symbolical meaning of the different exercises of the station, is given more fully and at considerable length in a little guide-book to the pilgrimage, the initials of its author, " B. D.," being only given. This little handbook was very defective and faulty, and is now superseded by the "Authorized Exercises" referred to in our last chapter. Richardson also gives a copy of the "Instructions," which directed the pilgrims in his time (1727). These "Instructions" are more diffuse and circumstantial,

but substantially the same as those given in the little
guide-book by " B. D." What I have said, however,
regarding the scope and effect of the different exercises
of the pilgrimage, sufficiently explains how efficacious
they are in awakening religious sentiments in the hearts
of the pilgrims, in producing feelings of compunction and
sorrow for sin, and in worthily disposing for the sacraments.

The sermons here preached are of the most practical
kind, and are followed by the pilgrims with the most
devout attention throughout ; so that we can safely say,
never did Gospel-seed fall on more congenial soil than
is to be found in the congregation assembled before
St. Patrick's Sanctuary on Lough Derg.

And even the ringing of the island bell, as it summons
the pilgrims to the various station duties ; the wild
screaming of the trumpet announcing the departure of
the ferry-boat ; the solitude, desolation, and surroundings
of the place—" all kindle in the soul feelings of awe and
reverence, and fill it with a keener sense of the power of
God, and of the strict account which He will require of
each one, when his brief term of life is brought to a
close,"—writes the distinguished annotator of the *Monasticon Hibernicon.*

Hence, seeing the peculiar efficacy of the exercises of
this pilgrimage towards renewing and increasing the
spiritual life, the sanctity of the place, and the graces and
indulgences there received, what wonder is it that the eye
of the pilgrim is charmed, his heart elevated, his faith
enlivened—nay, even his love for holy Ireland increased—

when first the Island of Lough Derg meets his view?
And what wonder is it that the Irish people should so
love this sanctuary? We love it on account of its asso-
ciation with the name of our National Apostle; on
account of the number of saints who here practised the
Gospel counsels of perfection, and whose names are in
benediction in the Irish Church ; we love it because of
the traditions which enshrine it in the Irish heart ; because
of the numberless sinners here reconciled to a life of
holiness, and who here "chose the better part;" and
finally, we love it because of the numberless graces here
received, and the blessings it obtains for its numerous
pilgrims, and because it excites in us lofty desires of
becoming holy.

As the island has passed through times of persecution,
and as its fine monastic buildings and noble churches were
demolished in the common ruin, we need not wonder to
find that most of the glories of its worship had fled during
this sad period, and that the buildings on the island in
the meantime were of so unpretentious a character. Of
late years a decided reaction has set in, buildings more in
keeping with the dignity of the place have been erected,
and the ceremonial of our holy religion is here observed
with more befitting splendour and solemnity. Extensive
improvements are also contemplated in the near future,
such as additional accommodation for pilgrims, &c. ; and
we fondly entertain the hope that at no distant day, the
religious generosity of the Irish race will erect here a
temple in every way worthy of this venerable pilgrimage.

The late John Donegan, jeweller, Dublin, fully realized,

as so few besides have done, the importance of this sanctuary, and its claims on the generosity of the Irish race. In the summer of 1858 he made a present to the sanctuary of certain church requisites to the value of £170. In connexion with this presentation, the following extract from the *Nation* of August 14th, 1858, will be interesting :—" John Donegan, whose munificence to the Catholic Church at home and abroad ranks him amongst the greatest benefactors to Catholicity, of whom we may be justly proud, has made the following valuable offerings to the chapel of Lough Derg—a remonstrance, chalice, ciborium (of solid silver), cope, veil, suit of vestments (cloth of gold), set of candlesticks, fine brass crucifix, bookstand, Missal (beautifully bound), thurible, incense boat, altar linens, incense, chime of bells, brass lamp, and wax candles. The chapel on the island, such a famous resort of pilgrims for many ages, stood in great want of these holy requisites, and priests and pilgrims shall ever more be bound to pray for this truly Catholic Irishman, whose gold and silver now adorn an altar annually visited by thousands. An inscription on the sacred utensils records the name of the generous benefactor, and states that they are presented to the Right Rev. Dr. M'Nally, Bishop of Clogher, and that they are to be henceforth the property of that ancient diocese, and to be used in the chapel of Lough Derg."

A large present of altar linens and other requisites was made to this sanctuary by the late Rev. Mother Beale, Superioress of the Convent of St. Louis, Monaghan, who in company with some of the sisters of her community came here on pilgrimage about ten years ago. Several other kind benefactors, also, have not forgotten Lough Derg in their charity, and we cherish the hope that their bright example will be followed in future by many others, until the sanctuary of St. Patrick's Purgatory shall have regained the celebrity it formerly occupied, and which at present it has such claims to occupy, amongst the celebrated places of pilgrimage throughout the world.

Before drawing to a conclusion, I should not forget to mention that at two o'clock each afternoon, the pilgrims' boat starts for Saints' Island, which is about two miles distant from Station Island; and a more delightful little trip can hardly be imagined. During the voyage the pilgrims while away the time most agreeably by singing litanies and hymns, and occasionally the sound of instrumental music may be heard. Having traversed Saints' Island, they start on their homeward trip, after having spent about two hours in this charming little excursion.

At seven o'clock each evening, immediately after the sermon, benediction with the Blessed Sacrament is given in St. Patrick's Church. For this ceremony the altar is very richly decorated with numerous lights and with a profusion of wild flowers gathered from the islands—woodbine, variegated heath, water lilies, various species of ferns, purple rockets, and with many other ornamental plants and flowers indigenous to these rocky islands, the odour and beauty of which are very pleasing to the senses. A choice choir, also, can be easily improvised from amongst the pilgrims; and, as there has been lately a fine harmonium purchased for the use of the island, both Mass and Bene-

diction are generally accompanied with very excellent
sacred music. And I may here observe that the ceremony of benediction, and the other ceremonies of our
holy religion here practised, seem to possess on this island
retreat a peculiar charm, and to impart a more solemn
effect than they do elsewhere.

In future we hope to see pilgrimages to Lough Derg
organized in most of the towns and parishes throughout
the kingdom under the direction of the parochial clergy,
the same as takes place to the Continental places of
pilgrimage. And in this every priest should take the
warmest interest; for we all well know what lasting
fruits of penance are produced by this pilgrimage;
how the rough stone is worn smooth by the generations
of pilgrims who here did penance ; and how many a sinful, sorrow-laden heart found here in this "prison" chapel
and on those "beds" of stone, light, and grace, and consolation. Nor can we estimate how much these religious
gatherings will tend to promote piety and fervour, and to
quicken the pulse of religion throughout the length and
breadth of the land. For proof of this, we have only to
look at Lourdes, and the many other holy places latterly so
much frequented.

And now, after having given what little information I
was enabled to collect concerning the holy island of Lough
Derg, I will briefly conclude by hoping that the fame of
this venerable pilgrimage may long continue to increase,
that its churches and other buildings may come to rival
the proportions and beauty of those fine monastic buildings which stood here during the ages of the faith ; that

crowds of votaries may long continue to feel before this sanctuary that interior happiness which its penitential exercises are so calculated to effect; and that the pilgrimage of Lough Derg may always remain as a fountain of mercy, grace, and salvation to the faithful children of St. Patrick.

NOTES.

Note to p. 20.

This legend of the serpent, and the change of the name of the lake in consequence of its death by "Conan the Bald," are referred to in an ancient poem called the "Finnian Hunt on the borders of Lough Derg." From this poem I extract the following stanzas :—

> "A serpent there was in the Lough of the mountain,
> Which caused the slaughter of the Fianna ;
> Seventy hundred or more
> It put to death in one day.
> "Fionn-loch Deirg was the name
> Of this lake, in the beginning, O Just Cleric [*i.e.* St. Patrick] ;
> But Lough Dearg remained since that time,
> From the slaughter of the Fianna on that day."
> *Transactions of the Ossianic Society*, vol. vi., p. 155.

Note to p. 33.

St. Patrick very probably visited Lough Derg on his way from Ballyshannon through Tyrhugh on to Tyrone. St. Patrick's sojourn at Ballyshannon is very fully described in the *Vita Tripartita*, Part II., where it is said, "St. Patrick went to Es-Ruaidh. He desired to establish himself there, where Disert-Patrick is, and Lec-Patrick. Cairbre opposed him, and sent two of his people, whose names were Carbacc and Cuangus, to seize his hands. 'Not good is what you do,' said Patrick ; 'if I were permitted to found a place here, the second to Rome of Latium, with its Tiber running through it, would be my establishment with its Es-Ruaidh through it ; and your descendants would be comarbs in it.'"

After leaving Ballyshannon, St. Patrick entered Tyrhugh, where Lough Derg is situated, on his way northwards. This journey is thus mentioned in the Tripartite :—

"After Patrick had blessed the Cenel-Conaill, and had left a blessng on their forts and rivers and churches, he went into the country of Eoghan, the son of Niall, across Bernas of Tir-Aedha into Magh-Itha." On this journey it is not unlikely that he visited *Teach-Dabheoc* on Lough Derg.

Note to p. 46.

Regarding the second St. Dabheoc or Beoan, of Lough Derg, the following extract from a legend given in the *Leabhar na h-Uidhre*, will be interesting :—"It happened that St. Comgall of Bangor despatched Beon, son of Innli, of *Teach Dabeog*, to Rome, on a message to Gregory [Pope, A.D. 590-604], to receive order and rule." A fabulous story is there told of Liban, daughter of Eachaidh, son of Muiredhach, having been metamorphosed into a salmon, caught in a net on the return of Beoan from Rome, and drawn by wild oxen from *Carn Airend* to *Teach Dabeoc*, where she was baptized by Comgall, with the name *Muirgen, i.e.,* "born of the sea." Another name for her was *Fuinchi*. This legend is given at length in Dr. Reeves' *Down and Connor*, p. 376. From it we can learn, making due allowance for fable, the parentage of St. Beoanus, or Dabheoc, the period at which he lived, and his journey to Rome to have his rule confirmed by Pope Gregory ; we also learn that a monastery stood here at that time, named Teach Dabheoc ; and that it was founded by St. Patrick, the name would imply, seeing that other foundations styled *Teach* were established by him. In proof of this may be adduced the following passage from the Tripartite Life, Part III., not to mention other similar passages :—"Patrick did not visit Ard-macha on that occasion, but went into the territory of Hy-Cremthand, where he founded churches and *residences*," the corresponding Irish for "residence" being *Teach, e.g.* Teach-Talain (Tehallen), *i.e.* the house of Thalain—*seu* Cillene.

Note to p. 67.

As the inscriptions at Lough Derg relating to St. MacNisse are so curious and interesting, I shall here add a few extracts, chiefly from Dr. Reeves' *Down and Connor*, pp. 237-39, regarding this remarkable saint. In the *Acta Sanctorum*, by the Bollandists, it is said that he was baptized by St. Patrick:—"*Quem venerabilis sanctus Patricius, Hibernorum Apostolus, baptizavit.*"

And of his education by St. Bolcan it is added :—"*Bolcano vero episcopo alendum atque docendum dedit.*"

Of his intimacy with St. Patrick, the Tripartite Life assures us, where it says :—"And MacNisse, of Condere, read his psalms with Patrick."

Of his pilgrimages it is said in the *Acta Sanctorum*, at the 3rd of September :—"*Perfectus autem vir factus, atque beato Patricio in episcopum suae gentis ordinatus, limina Apostolorum adiit, Jerusalem quoque, aliaque sancta terrae repromissae loca visitavit.*"

On his return home after his distant pilgrimages, he founded the church of Connor :—"*Connerense monasterium construitur, in quo usque hodie sedes episcopalis habetur.*"

The friendship of St. Brigid towards him is sufficiently conveyed in these few words :—"*Hacc de sancta Brigita dixit, quæ pro utilibus causis eum visitavit.*"

That St. Colman, Bishop of Dromore, profited largely by his counsels, we may learn from the following passage, taken from his life by the Bollandists, at the 7th of June :—"*Deinde saepe venerabilem Macnyseum Condereusem episcopum petiit, qui hospitum præsciens adventum eis necessaria jussit præparari. Ille itaque illuc perveniens, in omni hilaritate susceptus est: ibique paucis diebus mansit. Deinde inito consilio, venerabilem senem ubi locum serviendi Deo fundare deberet, consulit. Qui respondit: voluntas Dei est, ut in finibus Campi Coba tibi construas monasterium.*"

Note to p. 88.

Among the archives of England are certificates issued by Edward III., declaring that Malatesta Ungaro, Lord of Rimini, Fano, Pesano, and Fossombrone, and Nicolo de Beccario, of Ferrara, had performed pilgrimage to St. Patrick's Purgatory, Lough Derg. The following is a copy of this certificate, taken from Gilbert's History of *The Viceroys of Ireland.* " Whereas," wrote the King of England, "Malatesta Ungaro, of Rimini, a nobleman and knight, hath presented himself before us, and declared that, travelling from his own

country, he had with many bodily toils visited the Purgatory of St.
Patrick, in our land of Ireland, and for the space of a day and a night,
as is the custom, remained therein enclosed, and now earnestly be-
seeches us that, for the confirmation of the truth thereof, we should
grant him our royal letters.   We, therefore, considering the dangers
and perils of his pilgrimage, and although the assertion of such a
noble might on this suffice, yet we are further certified thereof by
letters from our trusty and beloved Almaric de St. Amand, knight,
Justiciary of Ireland, and from the prior and convent of the said
Purgatory, and others of great credit, as also by clear evidence that
the said nobleman had duly and courageously performed his pilgrimage ; we have consequently thought worthy to give favourably unto
him our royal authority concerning the same, to the end there may
be no doubt made of the premised; and that the truth may more
clearly appear, we have deemed proper to grant unto him these our
letters, under our royal seal."

Note to p. 95.

As an instance of the fame of the Purgatory during the fourteenth
century, may be noticed the following letter, to which my attention was
drawn through the kindness of Mrs. Atkinson, of Fairview, Dublin,
a literary Catholic lady of great ability.   Mrs. Atkinson writes :—
" This is a letter of St. Catherine of Siena, addressed to a certain
*Don Giovanni, a monk in the Certosa at Rome, who was sorely tempted
and in great trouble of mind, because he could not obtain permission
to make a pilgrimage to St. Patrick's Purgatory in Ireland.*   The
letter is a beautiful discourse on obedience and patience, and is of
considerable length.   In the end she strongly counsels the troubled
religious to surrender his own will in everything, but especially in
the matter which she has heard of from the visitor.   The editor of
' Le Lettere di S. Caterina da Siena ' (Fizenza, 1860), gives a short
account of the legend of St. Patrick's Purgatory in a note to this
letter, which is in vol. iii., and numbered 201."

Note to p. 112.

The only instance I can find of a parish priest of Templecarn having been also Prior of Lough Derg, is that given by the Rev. Mr. Hewson, who visited the island in the beginning of August, 1701. He states :—"On the ninth day (about two in the morning), the titular priest of the parish (whom they call Prior) puts them into the caves, one of which holds thirty, another sixteen, and another fourteen persons, the men and women separately."

Note to pp. 118-19.

With regard to the mediæval tales related of St. Patrick's Purgatory, and so eagerly seized upon by Protestant writers to justify their attacks against this venerable retreat, the following extract from Frederic Ozanem's work, intituled, "Des Sources Poetiques de la Divine Comedie," will prove interesting. After praising the perspicacity and erudition of Mr. Wright's work, this writer adds :—
"Mais pourquoi porter l'amertume de la controverse Protestante et la rancune Anglaise contre l'Irlande dans l'etude d'une innocente tradition qui ne fut jamais qu'un recit poetique, qui n'entra jamais dans les croyances theologiques de l'Eglise, et que les Papes ne laissireat pas introduire dans le Breviere Romain?"

Note to p. 170.

Amongst the clergymen who officiated at Lough Derg during the present century, and who are now deceased, we have only been able to ascertain the following names :—The Very Rev. Dean Bellew, P.P., Monaghan ; Dean Boylan, P.P., Enniskillen ; Very Rev. Patrick Moyna, P.P., Donagh ; Rev. Anthony M'Sherry, P.P. ; the Rev. Henry M'Phillips, P.P. ; Rev. Peter Gordon, P.P. ; Rev. Ross M'Mahon, P.P., Derrygonnelly ; Rev. Father Mullan, P.P., Errigle-Truagh ; Rev. Thomas Smollen, P.P., Blackbog ; Rev. Peter Miginn, P.P. ; Rev. Father Keown, C.C. ; Rev. Neil Ryan, P.P., Pettigo ; Rev. Patrick Carolan, P.P., Clogher ; Canon Cassidy, P.P., Dromore ; Rev. Charles Cassidy, P.P., Tydavnet ; and the Rev. Ardell Connolly, Adm., Clogher.

Of the clergymen still living, who ministered to the wants of the pilgrims at Lough Derg, I have been able to make out the following list, which, I suspect, will be found incomplete :—Very Rev. Canon

M'Kenna, P.P., Dromore, Prior ; Very Rev. Dean MacMahon, P.P., Carrickmacross ; Canon M'Donnell, P.P., Donaghmoyne ; Canon Smollen, P.P., Clones ; Very Rev. Anthony M'Geough, P.P., Ematris ; Rev. James M'Kenna, P.P., Brookeborough, who officiated as Prior during the seasons of 1867, 1875, and 1878 ; Very Rev. Dean Owens, Maynooth College ; Rev. James M'Quaide, P.P., Cleenish ; Rev. John O'Reilly, P.P., Blackbog ; Rev. Peter Maguire, P.P., Maguiresbridge ; Rev. Peter Byrne, P.P., Kilmore and Drumsnatt ; Rev. M. Carney, P.P., Derrygonnelly ; Rev. B. Duffy, P.P., Aghabog ; Rev. Daniel O'Connor, C.C., who assisted here during the seasons of 1869, 1876, and 1878 ; Rev. Joseph Woods, C.C., Clones ; Rev. T. M'Ardle, C.C., Eskra ; Rev. Eugene M'Kenna, C.C., Dromore ; Rev. Felix Hackett, C.C., Enniskillen ; Rev. Patrick Hackett, C.C., Aughnamullen, E. ; Rev. John Maguire, C.C., Blackbog ; Rev. William Downey, C.C., Pettigo ; Rev. Patrick Callan, C.C., Fintona ; and the Rev. Daniel Smyth, now a Passionist.

Note to p. 182.

In the year 1860 the station was closed, owing to the repairs and improvements effected on the island by the Rev. John M'Kenna, now parish priest of Pettigo. After these repairs had been completed, about the beginning of August in the same year, pilgrims were admitted to the island ; and, with the sanction of the bishop of the diocese, the station was continued till the 8th of September following, during which time a considerable number of pilgrims had visited the place. This is the only case I know of in which the station was kept open after the 15th of August. ╈ ╈

THE END.

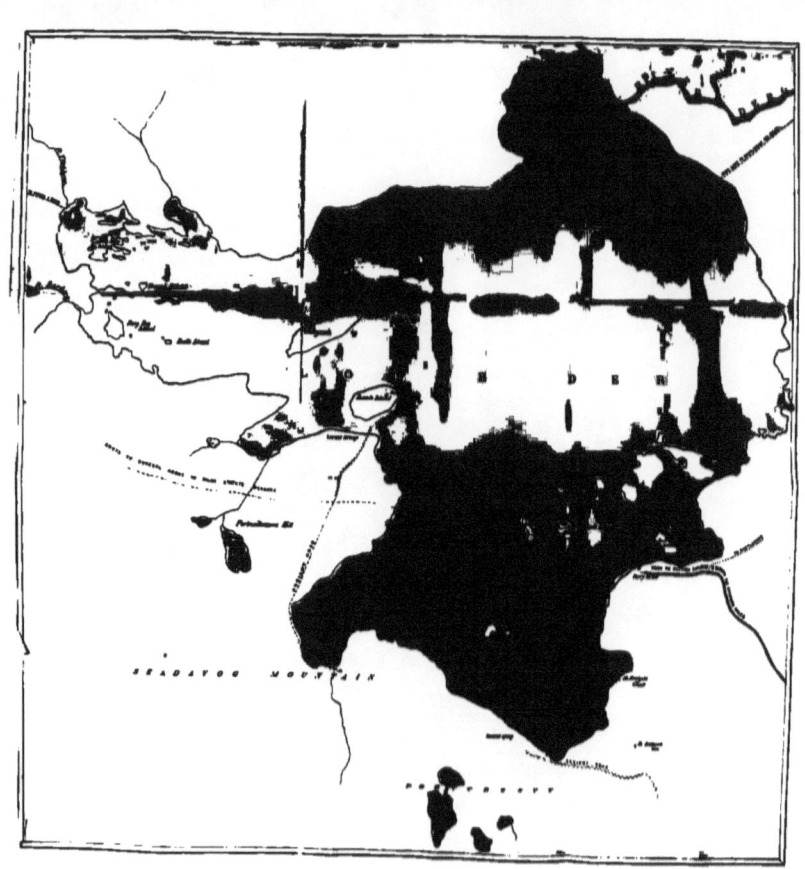